LOVES EVIL MISTER

KIERAN FORDHAM

authorHOUSE

AuthorHouse™ UK
1663 Liberty Drive
Bloomington, IN 47403 USA
www.authorhouse.co.uk
Phone: 0800.197.4150

© 2017 Kieran Fordham. All rights reserved.

No part of this book may be reproduced, stored in a retrieval system, or transmitted by any means without the written permission of the author.

Published by AuthorHouse 11/10/2017

ISBN: 978-1-5462-8456-7 (sc)
ISBN: 978-1-5462-8455-0 (e)

Print information available on the last page.

Any people depicted in stock imagery provided by Thinkstock are models, and such images are being used for illustrative purposes only.
Certain stock imagery © Thinkstock.

This book is printed on acid-free paper.

Because of the dynamic nature of the Internet, any web addresses or links contained in this book may have changed since publication and may no longer be valid. The views expressed in this work are solely those of the author and do not necessarily reflect the views of the publisher, and the publisher hereby disclaims any responsibility for them.

Chapter 1
LOVE WORKS IN MANY WAYS

Welcome to a story that many people have told in many different ways, but I thought I would write my own version of what I believe love really is starring two people who tell their story in their own way but it is so unique that you will believe every single line as you read. Francesco and Lena, were two very unique and special people who would share their romance for each other in many different ways, through your most well-known ways to your unusual ways it would almost seem to us unreal but they would make it look so real.

So you're wondering how they met? It came on a night like no other (they needed to make it look believable at the same time of adding coloured brown normally. But tonight these were in a very different style than what had been previously been seen. They had started singing and had a human quality that had not been noticed before and it became clear that this was a night that would go down in history talking stairs can't fault that one! I know right genius! Singing happy birthday and wishing them a very joyous farewell. She came further down the steps and was greeted by more enchanting to do's. It was a ball after all, picture this a talking and moving table full of amazing food goodies that would come to life. Everything from jelly beans to pieces of cake where on the move and talking to everyone coming through nothing is unusual as she went on to say: "Nothing is unusual. I really look forward to seeing what is going to happen next."

There is catch to this she doesn't know it yet but something is going to happen without her noticing things are to come to haunt her and this won't be the first time. Her friends followed on behind her and she couldn't help but want to come involved before she came in many of her friends saw her and wanted to have a chat which she was very open to "How's your day been?" "Aren't you missing something?" one friend stated she then thought what could I be missing? Tears then began to run down her face she knew what she was missing she was too afraid to tell her friends natural to think of course but we are hiding something here that we don't want her friends to know as well and that she is not currently aware of herself and that is going to be a surprise to all concerned, love has a trick up its sleeve! It's mysterious and as you'll see it's very cunning to say the least. It works in so many ways more than catches the eye that meaning the human eye.

Chapter 2

THE EXTRA CHANCE THAT WOULD CHANGE EVERYTHING

Stories come in many different parts but only this story could be told in many different parts, and can only be told in this way remember it's special. Coming back to the original idea we learnt that Lena had something special coming her way but she had many more obstacles before she could reach her ultimate destiny, this I promise we learn, but as you know to tell an amazing story you got to know the background story before revealing the truth right?

Would you have it any other way? Ha ha. The colour of the room changed when she entered from red to green, to purple to even a colour you don't even see (nothing is impossible right), so with that in mind it only goes without saying that when she went in she could only say "wicked" and not only once but many times she felt overwhelmed with excitement, that it could only be shown in one way you know when you have to show your feelings and there is no other way that you think of at the time it's logical, through many years of having great teachers many whom she had spotted dotted around the enchanted flowery, memory filled hall Lena knew the names of some not all. Mr Brads was a very beefy man with a ponytail at the back of his hair; he loved to wear black and white suits that sort of idea I joke of course he was one for many clothing accessories that were associated with ties and suit attire. Mrs Snick had her very brick red hair that she liked to show off at any time, which drew a large variety of people with what she had in her hair we can't give anything away now she could with a very slim figure she would always say how her husband followed on her gym going ways but had always struggled he had a big thing for food. She loved to go to the gym quite a lot daily if time allowed at home and elsewhere in neighbouring towns such as Forksworth, Knittingbourgh, you name it she went there.

Mrs Apple had a fetish for everything. Mrs Apple liked everything from eating apples to wearing apple inspired clothing it was a trend followed up by many a teacher it was amazing she had green laced hair like apples, also there was many a teacher with a fruity name. Mr Bear was a very different kettle of fish, however, though he was a very shy, skinny individual who could keep every thought he had to himself but was very open when he was given the chance. He loved the opportunity to know that he was very open to join chats at his leisure it made him feel good, and so many more to mention, there were so many! So many to name. She went through all she could remember and began reminiscing, it brought back a lot of memories she thought a lot of amazing memories: "them memories are incredible" them memories included times back in first year and fourth year when she would do some very awkward things like you're first performance in front of the whole class and how embarrassed she was she couldn't help but go "akwaaaaaaaaaaaaa aaarrrrrrrrrrrrrrrdddddd" she did this in a way that nobody would notice her doing it whispering it.

Her teacher back in 4th then goes you'll never guess "lol that has got to be the best thing I have seen someone do ever" Miss Apple knew she loved drama so it was only fitting to say "we definitely need to do a performance together sometime soon starring you Lena" exclaimed Miss Apple she could not deny this opportunity of a lifetime it would give that chance that she had always wanted that career she'd always dreamed of the life she had envisaged all along.

Everyone who noticed her immediately came over and spoke to her in regards to what she had been up to and the years that had been spoken about adding their thoughts of what they remembered they had many a thought that wasn't already known these were moments she would cherish for the rest of her life recalling this moment would be something she would never forget having gone from strength to strength with friends that she had from years past is something you treasure for years to come truly magical. As she chatted to her friends a face appeared who she liked and it was a face that she admired as soon as looked at it she couldn't help but want to try and reach him through the portal there was about three foot behind me and the swirling of the portal which lie over in the corner of the hall Lena gave it many valiant attempts with not one being of success her friends held her legs for support and tried themselves to reach what looked like several rings she put on her glasses and found it became clearer. What she didn't notice, however, was that it had a timed machine very close by it was on 5 minutes she knew she had to get out with haste. The time went very quick to very slow Lena and the girlies moved they ran like cheetahs you should've seen them the teachers ran not long after this.

Chapter 3

THE LOVE OF MY LIFE CONTINUED – THE PROM

The timer gets to 2 and a half seconds the use to be concert hall is deserted besides one person the one person had seconds before the whole of the school would go up into flames, Lena called out, "George!" The reply was muffled and quiet she had a minute and a half she had to find him they had many spots where they could check under tables under the stairs 15 seconds dangerous times if he couldn't be found.

"Check underneath that one!" Eight and a half seconds remained his voice became heard 4 and a half minutes remain this was life or death Amazon, Tina where in one area, Lena and Beatrice in another, The teachers we're outside by this time anxious. After searching 2 seconds remained he was found the hugs and the joy where big George and Lena were besties he was part of the posse so it was a relief to find him we had seconds literally to leave the building we exited out in the nick of time we jumped. I take another look at my love who I want to ultimately go and tell as he looks at me I want him you know when you look at somebody and you ultimately fall in love, you can't help but want to tell him! You have to do what you have to do :) before I reach him he disappeared in a very bright light but this light couldn't help change colour it went light blue, black and blue to finish off with. I was shell shocked there was so much to learn, where did he go? What was that light? Could I have something I don't know about?

    I very quickly turned back to my friends and I couldn't speak as we embraced in hugs and in future plans my friends after the hugs took a look at me and couldn't help but notice that something didn't seem right all the teachers turned very dramatically as they had some idea of what literally just happened in the distance to give you a rundown of what the prom looked like, it had tables with every single food imaginable although in the corner there was this portal which allowed unknown things to happen, such as what just happened, a person would go in and go out quite frequently without prior notice and it would disappear and almost explode and the school would almost be blown apart but stop was she being protected. They had returned back in after examination of the buildings later on that evening.

To get her mind off what had just happened Camilla one of her gals she would call her suggested a girlie night that evening. "I love the idea," she said, so without further ado it was made a date with this in mind she wanted to make her acquaintance to other people around her at this time in no time at all Lena met up with further friends and knew she wanted to dance. Her dance moves were the best especially with close knit friends she was wearing an amazing dress filled with sequences, and lovely other appealing extras that made it look beautiful everyone had mentioned coloured in red.

Now by this point there was a transformation in the way that the prom had automatically flipped and changed and transformed into a disco with disco lights you name it it was there and not only that but you had you're walking food NOT just walking but talking as well genius right you had you're wide range of alcoholic drinks and soft ones too to added food pizza, sausage rolls, carrots and hummus, crudities, pies, ice cream, you name it the hall had it imagine a hall which had just transformed into your dance hall setting with your choice of food snazzy stuff right.

Lena turned around all of sudden to her amazement she had to take two looks at it (I created it lolol) through the power of words can't fault that one right, the tables where now multicoloured they were spoilt for choice one beckoned them in their direction it called shouted almost "you know you want to come and sit with me" a wink was to follow lolol, another table called come and sit with me I have all the food you could ever want" I'm very attractive I can switch colours they looked on whilst in the very distance they saw a dancing table they were struggling to pick so much to pick from. They had a girlie conversation they had one of two tables in mind that they were debating the qualities of one girl wanted them all she was very keen to have them all it was the way they spoke that lured her to make the choice to have them all. They had made their decision they were going to go for the table that danced sorted! They walked over to the table as they walked closer the table seem to fade when they got there the table had vanished out of sight. Was that the same thing I saw happen earlier on? Was there a connection behind what happened earlier on to what had literally just occurred just now?

Chapter 4

THE APPEARANCE OF A FAMILIAR SIGHTING – THE BALL PARTY

Was that the exact same thing I noticed earlier on? Was the same person moving the furniture around? She thought for a fair few minutes to truly piece together who might be behind it and then she had a brainwave she knew, she turned around to the girlies and expressed to them who it might be, they agreed, surely it was him, the person who they were referring to was somebody who they had met at college previously, could he be playing a trick on them? They sat and had what could be described by them as an amazing banquet of food, they couldn't pick what to put on the plate, to add to the excitement the plates changed colour also from pink, to purple, to other magical assortment of colours they looked sharply around the room as through to say they spotted something or seen somebody they knew, the glow of a ball came spinning around the sighting they saw, it was a disco ball, and lights and noise it was party time they thought, with this in the forefront of their mind they guzzled their food down fast Lena was the first to eat, followed by Camilla, there was at least 30-40 groups of people in the hall during the prom 30 of the 40 people ate at that speed leaving 10 ate at their own allocated speed, it was about 10 past 11 when they had all finished eating the food they got, "you should've seen them" exclaimed one teacher after close examination of the students they got up on the dance floor and there dance floor moves were electric they were doing the funky gorilla, manoeuvre monkey and the jive this was the tip of the iceberg however they got down low too slow ha ha

It reached at least 3.30-4 in the morning and I felt incredibly sick and ready to pass out but you know when you have the moves you have the moves the colour by this time had changed to a very dark purple the disco had go off if you get what I mean! The last few hours had been like Saturday night fever FEVER! I say it was a Saturday silly me!. The room started to go early dark as if it was the lights had gone out, then I noticed something I had a very deep cut on my hands? Where did this come from she looked around at her friends and they shrieked in fear did this guy this person have super powers as they say we be able to tell you after the break wooooppp!!, I'm joking of course.

Chapter 5

THE CUT

This cut was unimaginably deep than you could of ever of dreamed of, her friends came to her immediate attention, seeking the relevant help. As she was out cold for at least 30 minutes, as they assessed the wound she had whilst still out they couldn't help but think who could have done such things it all happened so quickly, and without anyone else noticing or grabbing the attention of anyone else for that matter. Teachers and all that I can remember appeared as I awoke in a very secure hospital bed made especially with the help of my friends I couldn't of thanked them enough for the support they gave me that night, it seemed a very distant memory. My friends gave the picture of what exactly had happened that night I had fainted in such a way that I blurred out but get this I rewoke and then had more?

"Is this possible?" said Lena in a tone that was pitched to show that she had very little recollection of where she was and what she had done to as of the previous night. It was still a blur by the time she got to the afternoon, still laying in the hospital bed (created by her friends let's not forget) of course blur is an amazing band, she liked this a lot and had on repeat for the rest of her time in the hospital (you guessed it made by her friends) yours truly. The deep cut she had received had been so red in colour it was one of them cuts you don't see daily it was a very out of the blue type of one that couldn't be defined one that wasn't in the books one that you wouldn't see a person in real life have it was unusual sighting to see, as she lay there motionless through the half an hour she lay there thoughts were rushing through the 6-13 other people that had come over to see if they could assist or perform any CPR tactics on her.

After 30 minutes had passed she had got up in a moment of confusion spread over her face her hair was very ruffled but still the beautiful pink it had been at the ball the night before her blouse (dress) had distinctive traits of blood where she had fell and bloodstains had made there way to her dress as she collapsed. The blood had come from how hard she hit the floor. "That's a cut alright," stated Camilla.

Beatrice who lay on the floor helping with her performing her Level 2 that had been taught to her and all that she knew from previous years it was genius she was working like a pro!. "You're an amazing top friend I couldn't do it without you! I love you!" exclaimed Lena.

They went it to an embrace. "It really paid off your course I told ya," stated Amazon.

Amazon was a very caring individual and wouldn't want to see her friends get into any situations that would make them not spend a moment less together as there was a very close bonding between them all from a very young age they would remise about the memories long into the future and they were together whatever happened besties for life guaranteed!.

Lena had fully recovered in hospital 3 weeks later and been fully immersed with flowers and chocolate from family members and friends just to name a few (that of course of being Cadbury, amazing chocolate gotta love it wait that sounds a lot like McDonald's lol) Lena was incredibly thankful of the chocolate and all the great thoughtful presents she received, but there was still many more questions to be answered, did she have someone trying to follow her every move all to be unveiled next

Chapter 6

ANOTHER UNSUSPECTING TURN OF EVENTS UNRAVELS ITSELF TO LENA

Lena's birthday was soon approaching she was to turn 30 in 10 days the date was Sunday 5th July 1977.By this time and her birthday lied on the 11th meaning that she would have her birthday on the following Saturday. In the run up to her birthday she organised and planned to do quite a lot of stuff with the girls remembering of course she didn't have a boyfriend at this time and it began to play with her mind a lot she saw her friends with other guys and became increasing wanting of one to love and hold and cherish and be able to call hers. On the run up to Saturday she had planned parties, to include Friday, party night, and many other things to celebrate her 30th.

Friday had come around faster than she thought and the time to party came nearer and nearer every second she became excited and met up with friends to celebrate the moment, they went to the cinema, they went bowling, she was even told by her parents that they would be going on holiday very soon Sun- for 2 weeks in several destinations, her dad Trevor worked in a multi-award winning establishment named opening the door to success it had different elements to it and was growing fast he worked in only the highest rank of that business he ran the whole entire operation he was a director on the other hand her mum Roxanne was on the same wavelength as Trevor and was the owner of a place called Frimps they sold all types of very unique foodies everything from the food we saw in chapter 1 to more food to make you salivate Frimps homemade Golden delights these were a type of very edible cake glazed golden with a cream filling "these use to go fast" she said to her eldest as she recounts stories relating back to her day when Lena and the family which consisted of her, Trevor they had been happily married 35 years (we said it it all came from the horse's mouth lol) they had Lena, Lydia, Francois, Milly, Mick and Reese.

Reese was a very shy reserved kid who would stay very loyal to Roxanne, she loved her whilst the same was throught back it was a strong bonding between mother and son you couldn't of seen something more closer if you tried. Whilst Francois aged 10 soon approaching 11 was a very out there type of guy mirrored by his sister Milly they played basketball a lot and had shared similar interests they both liked to name a few cricket, rounders, football, tennis, swimming where just for starters, they enjoyed each other's company and shared the love they had for each other through hugging and spending time together and oh yes going to concerts together catching up on the latest acts pop acts of the time. Mick was your type of person aged 25 the oldest of the children who studied and enjoyed spending time out and about exploring and going on holiday where he could fully explore and be himself with girlfriend Rose they had been on many adventures and like Trevor and mum Roxanne they had been happily married from age 21 living four amazing years in each other's arms they were made for each other and everyone shared their love for them being together.

Lena was going to share a holiday like no other with an amazing family she had one request she asked her family a couple of weeks before the trip could one of her girlies come with her? Her mum happy obliged and they had not one put 2 come along her daughter's happiness meant a lot to her so Roxanne or Rox as Lena like to call her would throw a party just for her on her birthday not just one but 2 days prior, all her friends were down on Thursday they had party poppers, banners cake you name it, memories came back from previous times in fact flooded back she was shown a book by her mum to show when Lena was really young what they use to get up to this included a trip to Miami, a place they were due to go to this weekend, France when she was 5, America when she was 12, "spoilt" stated Roxanne "but I wouldn't have it any other way for my princess" she gave Lena a massive smooch on the cheek Lena did the same back now that Lena was away so regularly and conducting her own life Roxanne didn't get to see very much of her the rare trip here and there but not many. As she lived now not so far away but far away from her parents she was long overdue a visit she knew she had to see them with urgency now to be able to see her she couldn't be more proud. She reminisced baby photos of when she was young and showed how she had grown from the infant to the now adult. She took them one by one and the exact same effect happened from earlier on in the story she weeped and held her mum for support, she doesn't know it but she is going to need her mum now more than ever. Lightning struck outside leading to a 3 hour thunderstorm the sky was a very dark blue with clouds of rain that you know where going to be produced coming out of them, Lena and Roxanne continued to admire on but when Lena looked at least the fifth to sixth photo something had took over her mum her mum had menacing looking eyes and started to attack Lena clouds of rain? Thunder? Is this who I think it is?

Chapter 7

THE CURSED HOUSE

The whole house starting to move and Lena was being attacked by her mum who had a very zombified walk and had menacing black eyes she couldn't keep her eyes off Lena. "Mum?" shouted Lena. "MOTHER!" All her pleas were being drowned out by what appeared to be loud monstrous-like noise from her mum standing 2 to 5 feet away from her she returned to normal and then changed back.

"Lena I love you." The voice wasn't coming from her mum it was coming from a voice inside of her something had took over Roxanne. Lena stood rooted to the spot for what could be described as at least 5-7 seconds trying to fully understand who could be saying what her mum was saying but in a very familiar tone of voice to what she heard at the prom 2-4 weeks ago before she had time to think what to do something swept her of her feet and had left the house this thing that had swept her of her feet and into the air could only be described as a heavy force of nature which had a strong grip the whole house began to shudder and bricks began to fall within rapid procession of each other these bricks came from various parts of the house not all at first before Lena could reach the front door which was crumbling before her Lena tried to release the strong grip that he or she had on her this human was invisible :) although his grip or her grip was super tight he had one mission in mind and that was to get Lena who was crying and yelled mum to get her out of her moment with her mum she questioned such motives you could hear her saying "why the fuck is this happening who the fuck are you? I want my mum what do you fucking want with me" Roxanne had been completely taken over so much so you could see her wanting it to happen "take her" the force that had Roxanne made Lena or little Leni as her mum called her go backwards and forwards very quickly and hit many different close by targets causing as much havoc as possible it was very chaotic at this time you should've seen it.

By the time she had gained control there was no stopping the mystery human who was invisible and the mother who she could see from down below her it was truly terrifying she needed help and she needed it fast. Mickey and Reese had come back from footie that evening they both looked up and noticed how the house looked slightly different as their eyes travelled the room "Shit what's happened" gasped Mick in a state of shock Roxanne came out of her killing frenzy and saw to the boys leaving Lena to defend for herself her shoe had come off her hair was or had been thrown around leaving it very untidy "my hair" panted Lena when she looked up had changed colour and was not the colour it first was it changed to green not only this but her eyes had changed to a very dark evil black only for a brief moment then changed back the voice spoke again, "Lena Lena I love you loads I saw you in the prom and I couldn't help but want to be close to you you're the one I want you're the one I want to be close to I want you to come with me".

Lena had heard everything little thing and couldn't help by question why he would want to make her bang her head and mess up her hair was he the person I first meet and feel in love with or is he trying to kill me. Another part of her felt loved something she also destined for and feel a warm feeling and could only say "he's so cute but where are you" "I'm here I'm within your mum "you're inside my mum you don't have to be nervous come out and see me I won't bite. With this in mind he took Lena away from the devastating effect he left on the house and she followed to only feel a lot better and to be smiling knowing she knew who he was But questions still remained why do that?" What was the connection with my mum?

Back at home her mum had turned from being taken over still by the after effects of Francesco and developed after effects of the attack he had really gone for it. Francesco had a plan and quite a mind game at that he wouldn't reveal it to Lena not until she became unaware and when the time was right he would spring his trap and of course knowing Francesco it wouldn't be long till he did this. Roxanne as we go and find is a lot like her daughter in what she can do

Chapter 8

THE TALK

Talks come in many different shapes and forms but for this talk it was over something incredibly difficult to discuss it was there love you could be at this for some time you know what I am saying! For both parties involved which can only result in one thing a long in depth conversation with meaning and class. Francesco the invisible being and Lena who had her legs sprawled all over the show from being knocked around back at home 52 lighthouse road in Appleford her blue dress she had on had lots of noticeable pieces of leftover bits of debris from the crumpling house, Lena had took supplies with her as the rain had fell on her hair she had a sandwich to hand a ham one with cheese, lettuce you name it she loved it as a five year old child she would go to the greengrocers a lot back in 1962-1963 and head over to Rips the bakery in Appleford. The picnic basket or bag she had was full; she packed everything from chocolate, crisps to other delectable goodies Applefords finest she loved them she was one of them girls who couldn't do without her food intake you know what I mean Lena had been going to Rips for over 25 years! Wowzers she was a regular.

Lena flew further and further up bypassing many noticeable landmarks ones she knew. Francesco had done this through love but was it real? he showed some very interesting signs back at home everything from turning my mum evil to bashing me from wall to wall something didn't feel right it all tasted sour in taste Lena had her wits about her. She noticed her college, the shop she went with her besties. Clothes that rock fashion the outfit she got there was still in her wardrobe she had kept it still in tip top shape in mint condition. After 4 and a half hours of flying going over mountainous hills, rocky, dusty roads and terrain she had felt intensely dizzy almost ready to puck her hair by this time was almost falling off and it was set to fall off she had guessed her shoes had fallen off leaving her bare footed her clothing had been ripped off from falling into a forest close to Knittingborough a stone throw away from Appleford she had half of her clothing remaining showing her knickers and several marks on her face where she hit the rocky road down below Francesco stated "that was the best you looked real hot during all of that" murmured Francesco in a intisting sexy tone of voice she looked red faced "You're beautiful and I'd be lucky to have someone like you" the Scottish lass could only reply with "awww thanks you're so cute" it was one of the best 4 and a half hours ever!. Francesco showed his true colours with being able to show that he saw her for the person she was a truly amazing, attractive, lovely, beautiful as only Scotland could produce. He was truly gifted in the mind of Lena. Although a feeling deep still hadn't perished it was a warning she had a sixth sense a turn a twist by the way previous events had played out he had a trick to lure her in Lena was inside worried and outside an attraction that was strong love is powerful it has to be fought for!. Powerful love attractions is only right to be talked about in a park named romance in the great green.

Lena had entered what could only be described as her dream romantic picturesque setting for a date, which would be returned to it was her place like no other, the grass was covered to look like love hearts red in colour these could also talk like we saw earlier on in the book with the jelly tots. "They're so cute and small," voiced Lena in a loving tone of voice.

Francesco came out of his invisible state and took her hand and led her down a very stoney love rose filled garden this garden had a smell of love in everywhere you went it was so beautifully done that you'd want it as your own. Flowers of every colour imaginable were there they'd come towards you and let of scents you wouldn't be able to imagine, the colour of the sky changed colour it was yellow then it was purple the trees where all lovey dovey as well they connected and hugged, the love was big. The path rose up to create a bridge everything you could touch Francesco showed Lena why he loved Lena, he wanted to show Lena this his own imagination he called it imagination island sprinkled with love, "what you're thoughts" said Francesco "it's beautiful" exclaimed Lena, sharing the thoughts of Francesco, having kisses on her red rosy cheeks it was hard not to blush at the thought of this.

Even the seasons changed from zone to zone summer at first spring to winter it was amazing pigs could fly, horses turned to ponies there were rainbows it was colourful. Lena ran after what she described as a Scottish lass's dream a Border Collie to a Shetland Pony Lena adored them she was a little girl at heart she couldn't help but wanna relive them memories. Lena had a horse that her dad brought her when she was 5 years old and she had a dream to ride on them ever since not to say she hadn't rode on them before she had several she called one of them Princess that's a name you've got to love right? Memories kept flooding back Border Collies the Rovers kept at least 3 different types of pet at home they kept a Border Collie named Max, a pony not just one but 5 named racer, mater, tiger, Rudy and Cecil she was an animal lover alright. Pets where her life and she wouldn't had it any different if she tried. Lena looked over in the distance whilst having a very joyous time with animals that spoke her language and noticed what looked a lot a green figure standing in the distance she stood froze to the spot what had made her jump was Francesco creeping up behind her and scaring the living daylights out of her she was naturally curious by this point what's that over in the distance she asked, Francesco looked in the same direction and said "that's a leprechaun that is see her Lee he liked to call her whenever around her "this is the start of your dreams I know what you're in it to Lena" "Leprechaun pinch me I must be dreaming" Francesco pinched her she awoke to not being in a dream it was real as she had pictured it.

Francesco had put candles in Lena's absence on a very freshly mown, wet, hard rocky bit of grass that was shaped like a mountain, the sun beamed down upon them the seasons had all changed it was dark in one with snow, wet, windy and very thunder like in another so far away setting close to her. Lena had to take this all in once again looking at Francesco with glittery starry eyed eyes to looking at the other seasons taking place around her back at home it would of been hugely different. Francesco took out 2 wine like glasses out of a wooden basket he had in front of him, he set them out on a red and white table cloth like sheet he had although this wasn't in his bag to start off with he got from something prior to this secretly whilst Lena was away he ran he wanted to give Lena all she wanted to show how in love he was with her, he had orchestras not just one but 2 playing in the background with ponies on the clarinet and dogs on strings Lena laughed hysterically when show by Francesco she was in stitches, Lena had her dressed reformed by Francesco to show an amazing transformation of a white dress her hair was changed he looked her hair he golden, platted hair so he made it look incredible by styling it, it was more golden than ever she was without prior notice whisked away by tailored people to do her hair, nails, and to make her look incredible she came back looking stunning, Francesco had his own look as well suit of green and a purple tie he looked the part with his true love they were reunited but for how long?

Did Francesco have a trick up his sleeve, was Lena being played into a trap into something she couldn't get away from., Francesco had brought with him many the type of sandwich, sausage roll, quiche, dessert, starter, main as well it was bigger than first thought in fact it was huge he went all to town for this day that he could spend with Lena. Lena starting drinking and eating excessively she couldn't have been more hungry if she tried, and she knew it.

"Lena how have you been? I apologise for being invisible for so long." Francesco chuckled loudly.

"No probs," smiled Lena as she was halfway through a pack of chilli heatwave doritos.

"Lena I love you very you do know that right and whenever I look at you I can't help but want to kiss you and be a part of your life I did this for you," confessed Francesco in a look of love appearing across his face he lunged in and kissed Lena on her cheek whilst shoving in his 3 bit of quiche he was big on his quiche what can we say he loved food like Lena.

"I love you too and whenever I look at you I see my true love in your eyes," whispered Lena in a very heartfelt moment.

As they continued to eat Francesco's urge to ask more questions became more apparent the look in his eye turned from what was originally there to a very changed character he then started saying, "Lena, what are you doing here? You shouldn't be here. I tricked you," growled Francesco his face had also changed during the space of half an hour there very loved up relationship had turned darker? But how come? Is he the person I first saw when I came? Thirty minutes that's a very quick space of time for something to happen

Chapter 9

THE CLUTCHES OF FRANCESCO

Francesco had got up and before you knew it he had started chasing Lena around to catch her and try and put a very evil curse on her that would bring them closer together and bring them over to the side of Francesco. Lena ran as fast as her legs would take her; she grew increasingly aware that she had to find a way out. "Guards, seize her!" shouted a very disgruntled Francesco. The guards were at least 50 to 60 feet away from Lena; her white shoes were being lifted by the very thought of Francesco. Her brain was just about to be taken over until a very white light appeared in the distance; it was incredibly bright, it was going to be no match for the powers of Francesco and his imaginary army he'd imposed they had ways to take over the mind and soul that were more powerful than ever before.

Francesco took one very intense look at the white light and started assembling his army that grew in numbers. Lena had them up to where she was one guard kept a very firm on her as requested by Francesco Chris be his name. Chris continued to elevate her into the air this guard had ways of making every known moment back at the picnic disappear Lena became incredibly tired and started fading in the direction of Francesco immediately. The white light never gave up the white light showed what Francesco had and what he had originally saw in the moment he had with Lena, the white appeared to show several souls from heaven they were all dressed in white and suddenly cast what could be saw from all invisible guards present a yellow very hazy looking light which had sprung in the direction of Francesco showcasing his every flashback of what he had done everything from the picnic to very moment he saw Lena and feel in love.

"No!" shrieked Francesco, these are private memories he started to grow ferociously with rage. He approached them and with every bit of might, forced them out of his flashbacks as the sky battled from black to blue the white source would never give in he grew in power and within 5 minutes of fighting managed to move them out of his flashbacks and out of his head the white source moved with crying eyes as you would venture there would be everything you could ever imagine the world that use to be Franceso's any longer. Lena awoke with quite a start; she had guard bearing down on her she was too weak to move further before you knew she felt Francesco had got up and walked across having regained conscious he had a very strange trait about it that would enable to change back but before he could get to her, her mum came calling and what appeared was truly to be a miracle for Lena who lay face down on the floor with her arms sprawled all over the floor Francesco looked on and screamed, "Shit, what did I do?"

Francesco nursed her head whilst her mum saw to the rest of her wounds: "What happened?" argued Roxanne.

"Well," started Francesco in a calm tone of voice. Lena awoke back in her bed the next morning to recall the type of night that she had just encountered the house was still in a very broken state with bricks still falling around her she ducked on of them that came in close proximity of her only one fell on her head leaving her with an unsuspected cut on the head it was the same sort of cut as per the ball but this time a little bit more in deep, however, as it fell she noticed something quite odd it never missed it was aimed directly at her in the right area at the right time. It struck midnight and after carefully having her head examined by doctors she fell once more leaving a very worrying trend for her mum, Francesco had returned and he was ready for round 2 Lena wasn't going to get away that easily.

Chapter 10

FRANCESCO'S ROUND 2

This time round he came in and made an even grander entrance than before he had extra reinforcements this meaning extra guards and extra bodyguards to prevent attacks from all directions he was going to not get hurt this time around and he made sure of it he had one aim and that's to turn Lena on his side to whatever happened he had plenty to hand to last for at least 1 hour or more Lena looked up and felt she couldn't compete with she had got up in a complete daze she had quite a bruising to her head this was a day later or two she thought, the bruise to her head had left her in a confused state of mind. She was walking up with a very blurry outlook coming from her eyes.

Francesco neared closer and touched the right hand of Lena's as she lay there brought it up to where he was standing and used the power in his other hand to start performing what he had planned he touched his head got out his silver book in his pocket and started saying what he wrote. Lena awoke once again to the feeling of feeling quite strange Francesco had to be quick and sly about what he was trying to achieve he narrowly Lena by a thread she awoke and her hand went in the opposite direction to the way he wanted to go half a second more he would have done it Lena sat up and started mumbling words to find out who had hold of her arm it had had a strong grip although she had a pounding headache and a change she spoke and thought she started talking French and started doing things uncontrollably, she hit herself several times, once on the head and once on the nose she had never done this previously her nose felt incredibly painful more than ever before she couldn't stop the pain her brain was controlling her before you know it she was got up in her blurry eyed way and was being walked to the front door by her mind and her soul she was being led away from the hospital like this? By who? Her headache grew her eyes opened without being blurry the hospital was dark like the lights had turned off she couldn't see where she was going a voice spoke "Lena. Lena, guess who?"

"Fuck you!" shouted Lena.

"Fuck you too!" shouted Francesco. "I love you, Lena, and I am going to make you mine."

She was drifted off her feet, she became blind once more the power he had was carefully planned it was like he was trained to do this he was not going to let her out of his grip this time he continued to pull her towards the window where he was very close to the hospital began to shower with glass as he pulled her up. "What do you want with me please tell me?"

Two people tugged on her leg it reminded her of the time he had sent up into the clouds for that romantic date. It was her mum she had turned against Lena and started making sure that Francesco had his chance. Lena's whole body jolted and she felt a tad bit uneasy at this point. Her dad, her sister and brothers came to her aid as the hospital treatment she had made her very tired. Her dad made every attempt to get her sister and her brothers also took upon the same idea they too had ways they could change Francesco, who fought against them he had almost Lena to the bit where he was pulling and ultimate control.

Trevor started fighting against the power at the window Francesco he pulled his very own weapon what he liked to call daddy's fight against evil beings he would then let it do its thing it was known for causing someone to change minds and it was very effective it had travelled far and wide to seek its prey out. Francesco lay at the top still grabbing hold of Lena, who was halfway towards the window nearly in the clutches of Francesco daddy's fight against evil beings time was running out 5 seconds remain Lena had no control of herself her body went with the flow it was the sword against Francesco 3 seconds remained it was intense by this time everyone looked on in ore her brothers, and his sisters looked up they felt a mixture of fright, tears, their hearts leapt there dad stood motionless he froze, 2 and a half seconds remain the sword got to where Francesco was the sword took one glimpse at Francesco they looked at each other leading to a very sour taste in the air the first shot came from the sword Francesco looking red in the face about now with anger and want for something he wanted action he was getting impatient and became increasingly more and more violent he totally ignored the sword and became panic ridden he upped the antic and took to increasing the power he had on Lena.

The sword was not having this 1 minute remained he went for Francesco he went inside his brain and tried to discover what was truly happening. Francesco reacted in moments of the sword entering his head he used every bit of might he had to get the sword from changing his thought patterns he took one hand and managed to lodge out but by the time this had happened he'd already been changed the sword reigned victorious. Francesco loosened his grip on Lena and she fell with her sister catching her she was in need of hospital treatment the impact he had was great. Francesco came immediately to the action of Lena who was none the wiser.

Chapter 11

THE DATE

Lena was out for quite a number of weeks prior to the standoff with Francesco it was getting dangerous he could be around any corner and no one knew what he had up his sleeve next when was he going to run into Lena next. It was 3 weeks before she officially woke up fully recovered her family around her Trevor, Roxanne and her brother, sister where all around her for support, Trevor gave her the rundown of what had happened, she felt like she had woken from a dream the way it was told it couldn't be denied it sounded like a dream playing out in her mind.

"Wow a lot happened whilst I was out and cold," mumbled Lena as she was getting back to her old self and getting familiar with her surroundings once again at home and at Reese Woods hospital south of Appleford. She made out some things as she began to fully be able to see once again she could make out Trevor's locket he wore around his neck and Roxanne's bracelet and Mike's bag he had on his back with his cool boy stuff and her sisters beautiful hair she had the finest black hair ever.

Lena was escorted into a black limo located outside the hospital very slowly due to still feeling a little tender from the previous night's going ones. Lena was in the back seat of the limo when she had a vision which she wasn't aware of that would come true in a later on period of time, she saw what looked like a figure appear in her mind like Francesco she was scared to start off with due to what had gone on, then out of nowhere appeared a part of the thought that she thought she would never have they went out to dinner and candlelit at that it was amazing back in them clouds where they had the picnic that dream would turn into a reality sooner than she thought she had voices in her head say the next line "I am going to have a FUCKING candlelight dinner with my one true love" she had shouted with excitement "I can't FUCKING wait" she screamed in the limo her heart was racing she was excited at the same time nervous "Shit" she whispered she had never been on this type of date she started to boogie to the era of music really loudly back at home on their famous couch the famous blue colour the weeks she had been out the house looked brand new could this be Francesco's doing?

She decided to have a house party to celebrate the joyous occasion she invited the whole group of girlies they made a day of it they went to the cinema, explored areas they might not have explored before, and explored so much more. When they were coming back from the cinema and lunch Lena had another vision as the girls were all together holding hands Francesco appeared in her thoughts again, however, this time it was a change to what she saw earlier on he had turned it around she pictured a wedding for him and her that had one of his plots intertwined into it "shit" her face went red at the same time she started shaking uncontrollably something allowed her to think in this way.

"What's wrong, babe?" worried B "Motherfucker has his took over your mind again Lenannypoo cock" panted Camilla, Lena was a statue she started talking like Francesco "Lena is mine! Woahhh! she turned around to her friends and her facial features looked like Francesco they had exactly the same nose, coloured eyes as what Francesco would have.

Lena the new Francesco looked at the sky and changed the weather from the sun to rain very dark colours ascended from up above the girlies ran away Lena changed back. "Girlies, I'm not sure what is happening Francesco must have control of me in some way there is a bit of him in me," she fell and vomited within seconds. "Fucking hell" croaked Lena.

She saw the vision of their wedding he had planned although he had twisted it Lena was begging him to marry her she was begging for mercy she was at the legs of Francesco "I will" obeyed Lena he was playing mind games. Her whole body was under Francesco's power they moved down the road going from pavement to road very quickly cars where dodging her by metres Francesco changed to his original self and was back on the pavement his inner spirits had moved but a bit of him would be always be connected to Lena the love was there Francesco himself had moved out of Lena leaving her to question his state of mind she became increasingly worried as anyone would she could see the spirits descend on to other bodies she could see invisible stuff anything Lena could see Francesco saw too that was her theory she mentioned to family and friends with this in mind she was going to pursue the idea she had in the limo earlier she was very weary by now.

Francesco was waiting in the restaurant that was pictured in her dreams Lunch at Frankie's he waited there with his suit and famous attire he sit there like nothing had happened Lena looked down at herself and was wearing the dress she had on earlier on it had no cut off bits revealing anything it was all clean she was a split second away from her restaurant she had visualised she went through a green handled creaky door handle when she entered she had a cold feel come before her she saw the person that had took over her not so long before now Francesco she walked towards the front door Francesco stopped her that part of her mind that was controlled by him took over at this moment and took over to the table

"What the fuck do you want with me, arsehole?" quizzed Lena.

"I want you, Lena. I want you to love me, Lena," clucked Francesco.

"You tried to kill me, motherfucker," cursed Lena. "You almost killed me back down 57th street, you cock."

"I didn't mean to I just more of you," pleaded Francesco as he brought Lena closer towards him as he went in for a kiss Lena restricted the urge but Francesco had the powers to set his affairs in order he got what he wanted both mouths connected they kissed and it was the best for both considered Lena was under Francesco control there was no going back was Lena going to forgive?

Was Lena going to reunite their relationship? Lena had a big decision to make after the kiss she looked at Francesco in a no I can't do this because what you have done before but Francesco had one more trick that he knew would get Lena on side remember he had Lena's brain he was totally in control of Lena and her every move he offered a dance she was just about to leave he lured in by taking over her brain once more "you know you want to dance I love you you love me remember" spoke Francesco from Lena's mind she knew she did she went in for the dance they started taking each other hands and each other waists and she had memories once more from the time she was at the ball they sung along to the music and had a really great time together Francesco kissed Lena once again she blushed this what she wanted she had this in her throught this was her special moment Chic - Le freak started to play and Lena was busting some moves Francesco got jealous you should've seen him it was great to watch love at first sight it was the cutest thing it was the era of amazing times ahead 1978 and without a shadow of a doubt 1979 just like at the ball in chapter 1 it was the exact same look it matched they begun to do a routine that they had practise as seen in Lena's wedding fantasy they did ballroom dancing although something didn't add up he didn't do as it was first pictured before the evil scheme begun to take the form of what she had in her mind very different he started doing the moves like in a different direction and started taking some odd turns like she saw down by 57 street she fled Francesco had turned back I lied to you his facial mask came off only to reveal another Lena where was Francesco at this point a loud thud came from one of the walls in the restaurant she turned she felt the full force of Francesco as the whole of the restaurant turned into Lena "what the fuck is going on" cried Lena. The wall crumbled from around her she had to find an exit and fast Francesco had gone for Lena once again? How was she going to escape this time?

Chapter 12
LENA'S BIG EXIT PART 1

Lena was not holding back on any account she was not going to let Francesco get to here she had ways as proven to get him out of her mind to her arsenal she had her dad not too far away something that Francesco didn't have, Francesco also didn't have a mum she delved into her pockets in secret whilst Francesco was unaware and took out a silver cell phone which her dad was able to give prior to leaving the house before Francesco had full grip of Lena it was in time of emergencies that it had to be used it was one of them times in fact it was her dad who came to the rescue in the hospital bit through the phone the silver genius it was great when times became tense and needy.

Lena farted she was that nervous and not just once but 3 times over it was tense stuff she was sweating more than you can imagine haste she tried to find every available exiting point she could before she had a chance through a certain someone catches up with her, Francesco had found her in her hiding place she moved very fast once again Francesco had got a grip of her leg very tightly she tried to let go but then took hold of her head and tried to seize back control. A force from behind had took hold of Francesco as well you should've seen it "Fuck off" panted Lena in an attempt to get Francesco of her "I will take back fucking control once again" demanded Francesco he took his hand and placed them on Lena's body so he had complete control so she couldn't escape. "Dad help" pleaded Lena to her dad who was desperately trying to take the control of Francesco away from Lena and fix the restaurant falling shattering glass feel from every known part of the 60-year-old restaurant. Everybody took cover with immediate effect injuries where by this time coming a common occurrence for Lena, the other people in the restaurant had very serious injuries as well "I'm going to take over your brain Lena, and the minds of your dad and mum, through the power of taking your mind I will make you see what you are fucking missing out on bitch you love me I know you do what do I have to make you see this" explained Francesco" "you're trying to kill me why? Motherfucker" quizzed Lena.

Lena had the voice of Francesco take over in her mind Francesco connected with Lena again flashbacks occurred in light of this Francesco had managed to captured pictures of when she was younger and how when she was in school she dreamed of this and so much more to happen everything from the dance to get caught up in this cunning plan of his she was being dragged and knocked when she made an attempt to get up back in the power of Francesco she got up and feel consistently allowing glass to hit on her head by this point she had a massive graze on her head. Trevor run frantically to get Lena out of the mind set of Francesco he had double the strength of last time he hid in a desperate attempt to escape Trevor Trevor and Francesco when at it at full blow gaining back the power that was needed to get Lena out of her seized back control from Francesco he got back out daddy's fight against pure evil once again and began fighting and winning back the control. Was Lena in Francesco's grip now or would daddy save the day?

Chapter 13

THE FIGHT TO SAVE LENA PART 1

Lena was still in hiding being brainwashed by Francesco. Trevor knew he had to act fast it was a life or death situation. Trevor moved in and started using what would be to his daughter's advantage he stepped in closer and took to taking back ultimate control Francesco recalled what had happened last time and came prepared he was not going to let Lena's dad have the upper power so to speak red, green and yellow could be seen coming out of his weapon he would use the red would bounce straight of him the yellow would cause a bit of his mind to be taken out "holy shit" screamed Francesco as a bit of his mind had gone he had forgotten nearly half of what he did yesterday with this just happening he couldn't help but want revenge he upped the ante he had a one of his very powerful sword himself "You think you can do that to me motherfucker think again" He pulls out his very own source of defence this one was ten times as strong as his "You wouldn't do that you evil bitch" "pleaded Trevor "Oh I would I am going to make Lena love me and you seem to be getting in my way" cried Francesco.

Lena had got back up by this point and his inner character had vanished and seeked refuge in another it would only last for half an hour. They came and went through the wrong person. "Guys, what are you doing, you're meant to seek refuge not in me but in another body what's going on, what's fucking going on?" protested Francesco. The spirits had played havoc by the time. "No!" screamed Francesco.

"Woahhhhhhhhhhhhhh," fantasised Trevor. Lena had become very dizzy and whenever she was taken over by Francesco she would have the world seem different she came into the light of Francesco.

"What the fuck you doing up you're meant to be taken down?" questioned Francesco.

Francesco tried everything to get back at Lena to keep her mind under his control this was easier said than done Lena would not allow her beautiful self to get beaten by Francesco again so whilst she was done and out cold she lied about being took done by Francesco she had her eyes closed to trick him. Francesco was easily fooled but in some cases not in this scenario he was.

"I have to tell you… you didn't easily get to me, dickhead," laughed Lena her head still was in quite a lot of pain from being hit with the glass a bit was sticking out of her head and bite of glass were still falling from the crumbling restaurant.

The lunch, dinner, and tea restaurant the 24-hour opening eatery was falling quicker than you could say fast they had to get there asses out of there speedy. Trevor by this point had part of his brain gone and Francesco had turned further to allow further parts of the restaurant to come down. Lena joined her dad two against one only one could win Francesco used his weapon and came forward and started attacking Trevor directly with it to have maximum impact he did the exact same to Lena the sword pierced through her chest to allow Francesco's mind thoughts to go back into her and through her brain he even had a backup to ensure it would not fail there was not just one know but 3 of him there all continued to use Francesco's mind control he'd even updated his kit from failing last time he had a chocolate bar Chocopower, he had mind controlling gun which would get her to believe that being with Francesco rocked. Trevor had to think on his feet Lena came up with a plan of action she whispered in her dad's ear and that the same time of kissing and hugging for a brief second and brought him to the side to cover they put both what they had together and came back up to face Francesco it was bigger than first thought she had a cat that transformed into a monster "you pussy" voiced Francesco he too transformed into a big monster although it wasn't him it was one he had in an orange trunk he had to the right of him. Both monsters fought out at each other each growing in size at an alarming rate "ha ha ha" laughed Francesco the monster had grown one bigger than he did before when a certain guitar played with gentle played strings like that you would of believed that he would decreased in size but with the strumming that took place he grew and didn't stop compared with the mars they had a flute and a higher up the scale instrument drums they would play this and it would make sure that Francesco didn't stand a chance.

A very few minutes before the fight came to a head and with the restaurant almost down and out the portal appeared once again the same size and colour. Lena made it out before Trevor, the colour grew brighter and brighter and brighter they were blinded by this and started to get sucked in by it "ah not so clever now are we mars bar" "Fuck you prick" she both her hands up to gesture this to a very distant far away Francesco, the light would not getting into the eyes of Lena so much so it strained her eyes she became blind and start to bump into things as a mystery source believed to be one of Francesco's men Rufus. Rufus had very scruffy black hair with a very large build of a body with a moustache like the Pringles man or like a Mexican guy lolol all completed with multicoloured eyes blue and red red to indicate trouble you would get him mad and he would make it known to you then you had Piero very slim of build muscular in shape he loved to keep in shape regular gym sessions working out at home he too had a strong connection and bonding friendship since being very young beings no one knew that they were going to form at this very minute in time.

Lena tried to turn back time to turn back to the point where it would of gone wrong for

Francesco she had glasses she liked to call Lena's visuals she managed to take it back to the time 1976 when they had the prom he was young and very confused.

"I do believe I have you in my control," insisted Francesco.

"Fuck off!" bellowed Lena. Lena got to the point with her glasses on where she had many a reflection come at her within seconds his past was something that had to be questioned. He started to chuck from his golden encrusted jacket he got out when started memory balls that would allow Lena to stop was she was doing Lena caught it and chucked with force it back in his direction the space between Francesco began distancing her mother returned and bridged the gap whilst Roxanne fought off what now was more than monsters ghosts too! Scary times lay ahead Lena was drawing into a tight spot the portal was where Francesco came through and so many more but where did it lead? It was incredibly dark in there and seemed deserted all they could see was the rings that were visible from the prom days, however, there were voices it became spooky Lena was determined to learn nothing scared her she had to get to the bottom of this but this was just the start of something that was up and coming for her

Chapter 14

THE FIGHT TO SAVE LENA PART 2

Lena was being sucked in and she felt powerless but she had sources what she could call upon if she needed it these were needed now more than ever at this very minute luckily for her she had already build one bigger than Francesco's by a long shot. Francesco's monster was about half the size of hers but whilst she had her back turned there was no telling what was going on Francesco had used his growing powder or as he liked to refer back to as his mind controlling gun. This gun would squirt out different colours to mean different things for example red and a very dark shade of orange would indicate that he wanted to be able to take over your mind although with this it could backfire at any time, although with Francesco there was a secret ingredient he added to make it go all the way his voice would be added whilst the opponent was aware of it so with Lena for example he would add more of his voice to spice it all up it didn't fail.

By this point with Lena being so far away and Trevor being within 2 feet from her, Francesco knew he had Lena a little but not fully as Trevor managed to take over a piece of his brain which he took back by striking at it exactly the same time there was only seconds between both. Francesco with half of his brain could still voice what he wanted to happen he whispered telling his inside spirits evil creatures these were these do grew it was so silent that not even Lena could hear it her hearing was perfect crystal. Having had an element of Francesco inside her she would not miss what he was saying she turned red blood spiriting out of her eyes and mouth Francesco looked horrified. Half the spirits resided in her and had changed colour Lena was spinning in one big circle the restaurant goers still in hiding. The police were very quick to turn up having had phone calls but the calls were muffled when there tried to call in the time that her watch had turned back to was the first calls. The police were determined to get it but time would not allow.

Francesco caused more fire to bellow causing the gap to widen. "Shit," cried Francesco, "wrong move." However, when he made the call to his inner soul spirits they had made their move to Trevor they took control of Trevor. "Yes this is what you get when you miss with me, Lena, you fucked with me now I'm fucking with you," shrieked Francesco.

"You will get your compance you don't have a dad or a mum I know love do you you've tried to kill me," questioned Lena with Francesco. "You son of a bitch!" screamed Lena.

Francesco very quickly at this remark came charging like a cheetah he was like a hyena towards Lena how was in a fiery inferno, ambulances, fire engines tried entering they never gave up, people paced the street thinking about love ones Beatrice sat outside breaking down she had a daughter in there she smashed the glass but was refrained back the time wasn't right for entering, Camilla knew Lena was in there and the hands of Francesco it was going to take a hero to be able to get here out. The sky outside was very much normal with all the action taking place in the restaurant. There were frantic attempts to come with a plan the rubble was piled one upon another as the restaurant was on its last feet, there was at least 1 hour till it became deadly. Camilla and Beatrice noticed something flying out of the sky at this exact moment it was green, very spiky and slimy it was the arch nemesis of the beasts that B could see in the fiery, debris filled restaurant his name was Glorimpus, to indicate good things on the horizon, he walked slowly and cautiously into the whirlwind of what was a very disastrous scene anything could happen and at any minute it was an unpredictable set of affairs.

Francesco had set up 3 invisible traps for anyone trying to get one up on him the first was no match for Glorimpus he set his own trap and was clearly a level headed monster ready for anything, the trap to give you an outline went a little something like this it was full of the power to take over even a monster's mind, Glorimpus took one step back as a precaution, but managed to outwit the mind power. "Gawahhhhh!" chanted the monster as he hit his chest this could definitely his floppy green skin flopped all around you should've seen it he got to the second trap seeing the way he got past the first with his manliness and true bravery and will you would think it would be no match but Francesco went in 3rd gear for this one. He would make sure that the higher you went he wouldn't be caught out this time he had two of the same monsters as him, to add to this he had two armed soldiers protecting base from Francesco who was 50 feet further away from these soldiers they shielded the way past they were locked into whatever Francesco requested they have walkie talkies. To top this if he wasn't in enough danger already fate was staring him in the eye; everyone by this point had an incredible amount of brick rubble and glass on them 40 minutes remained Glorimpus knew he had to act fast hero was his second name Glorimpus hero lol you can't go wrong there.

Chapter 15

THE FIGHT FOR LENA PART 3

Glorimpus came forward cautiously with speed he had been fully trained up in Roarville this was in totally place to where lie Francesco they were a feet between each other longing to always fight to see who would be the best Francesco's cloud was always a lot darker but as you know he would switch from good to evil quite frequently. On his cloud he would be hatching his next step to be able to brainwash Lena into being his and would frequently see to going down from his cloud flying. He would have cameras spying on Lena's every move this time he had back up that were powerful. You couldn't make it up they had been trained by the strongest power in Appleford Francesco the noble, great the almighty source of the darkest evil you could ever of imagined.

Back inside and Glorimpus was still trying to fight his way past Francesco's traps he'd almost got through part 2 but part 3 was the ultimate in a line of 3 with his big meaty claws he ripped into the soldiers they were almost down everyone on of them besides 2 they were built with the utmost attention in creating and bringing them to life, there metal seemed stronger more tighter and a lot more resistant it could definitely tackle any shot handed to it. It fired grenades the size of giant baseballs. The first one missed Glorimpus went from one side to another in the direction in a bid to miss them. A couple more fired and got him, however, his skin detected it fast and the next thing that happened was something quite spectacular quite breathtaking honestly fantastic the missile shot came out of his body and back in the soldier's metal guarding for his body it was a quick fire moment full of action and as everyone stopped to see where it would go there was even more silence in the air the bullet of be shot back hit him so hard it was unreal it went straight through the metal and he feel. A very strong blowing of wind came through at this particular to lead everyone to remain silent. It wouldn't be till about 20 minutes remained would panic set in.

Everything was going at such a pace it was unreal everyone was running into everybody to escape 15 ½ minutes remained and it couldn't be more life or death if you tried the atmosphere was in need of something urgently. 10 ½ minutes remained Glorimpus followed by friends who had now arrived for backup you had Humpimpus he was the colour of blue a very light blue at that he had managed to bulldozer down with Glorimpus the 2nd trap of Francesco. To follow on behind him you had Sweetpeaius she was lovable and very fluffy she had super powers to distract the slight obstacle in the way allowing the fourth in the gang to do his thing you had Gorgimpus his power was whilst Sweetpeaius his love for monster to monster was to protect the group and especially Sweetpeaius if anything happened to her he would turn pretty mad up in monster land that's what you call monster love.

He cut across every known guard left just with a swipe of his finger through not being successful in previous monster battles though through practicing he got there of course practicing you can achieve anything. It was ace to watch he broke through the barriers that the soldiers put up before them Gorgimpus being the brave person he was celebrate being victorious just before seeing the third obstacle of cunning Francesco's plan. This was his last hurdle to reach him as a person admittedly he was sweating in the bucket load literally you had to have a bucket nearby he looked shell shocked and frightened, however, his inner spirits were determined "get him!" They yelled they created a bubble around Francesco get sucked in and you'd know about it you'd be truly in the world of Francesco you'd be sucked all the energy out of and you would potentially die.

Gorgimpus took one step at a time noticing and hearing the signs of danger, however, he had all these people to rescue his walk that was slow turned faster and faster speed walking to running. All the other monsters followed on used all their super powers working as a team they had to think of a high speed plan 7 and a half seconds remained before they risked getting caught up in the mess people were at the heart of what they did. They decided upon something risky but went for it nonetheless they begun with the bulldozing effect as they knew it would be very effective and you knew he would break through anything our Gorgimpus then Sweetpeaius gave it ago with her ways of percussion she tickled and striked up a conversation that was Sweetpeaius all over it worked. Just to give you a rundown he tripled the guards, the monsters, the power to get you in his mind, he'd even had like mini tornadoes that would allow you to get sucked up again it was deadly however there was a trick to stopping it and only Glorimpus knew "Grand back" gurgled Glorimpus. Once again the tornadoes swirled back in Francesco direction "Sorry boss" the tornado caught Francesco from his foot and lifted him from his feet up but escaped before he reached the top. "Ha ha you didn't get me you have made me incredibly mad time to get my own back. The incredibly toxic and deadly drawn nearer and took hold of only 1 monster leaving the others but Francesco knowing he was failing drew a bigger circle this time it reached them but in light of being trapped the three like they always would helped each other escape free Roxanne run further forward with her legs taking her and running as fast she possibly could. Her white shoes fell victim to the circle of death.

Francesco had two sources of uncontrollable power which he showed no signs of backing down. One second remained it was imperative that they knew that time wasn't on their side.

Lena was being pushed further and further in the dominance that Francesco had was so overruling that when he when tightened his grip it was in an effort to cause her as many injuries as possible she had cuts and Francesco inside her system. Down on the floor Gorgimpus was struggling he tried to fight it but what he didn't release that Francesco had took his every power source his power had gone he had his monster slimy leg being taken up in a net plus he was in bubbles. The other monsters tried to gain entrance into the bubble everything that was taught was used but he was losing and Francesco had took the ultimate control you could the ultimate cries being muffled out. "Gy Gnoster Griend Gno!" Everyone mucked in in a rescue attempt but Francesco was determined to reign victorious and despite their best effects he fell and died "Gno" another wave of silence descended across the whole of the restaurant. Seconds remained but in them remaining seconds he switched back and the whole of the force of

Francesco had gone leaving Lena to fall back down to the floor with a hard crash every bit of the restaurant was still damaged but the police and other emergency services emerged and started an ever growing urgent search for survivors bricks shattered glass and other bits of debris lie on the ground.

Chapter 16

THE SEARCH

Francesco stood there waiting for police to intervene and arrest him he knew he had to get rid of his inner evil spirits somehow. "Never, never," they murmured back from inside he managed to entangle them inside a bottle that he found with the spirits voices inside he opened it up and the voices spoke one you know voices that only anyone with a mind like Francesco's would hear. They spoke at him very quietly and in a whisper these weren't just filled with voices these were filled of memories from Lena's. The police ventured further towards him he stood there knowing what to say next "was this anything to do with you" calmly spoke one police officer. He was to just about to lie through his teeth or tell the truth, anticipating and carefully thinking and monitoring his next thought he decided to lie, his hand uncontrollably wobbled as he gestured towards a girl lying on the floor. Covered in very thick red blood. The police walked forward but as they did so did Francesco through secrecy and being witty he had turned the restaurant into a snow filled ice rink the police proceeded forward but slipped he had made it so slippery the ice was so thick it broke apart. Bit by bit the ice swallowed up the policemen the policemen had vanished were had Francesco took them his evil screething plan worked you see he had put on a face to think he was guilty however through the few minutes that the police came forward he had done this and darkness caved in around him. His eyes gave way to a red colour once again. Lena had got up but how? Anybody would've thought she be dead but no it wouldn't of seemed was it something we didn't know about? Is there something you're not telling us Lena?

Chapter 17
THE MANY FACES OF FRANCESCO

Lena got up the indestructible being she was and observed what was going on due to be on that part of the floor for some time she was a little bit hazy in memory so it would take some time but she knew what she needed to do by having Francesco's every up to date known thing that he would of had going on his mind at that time and before. The first thing that had to be done is that whatever happened she needed to follow the every demand of Francesco remember he had gone but there were still men and guards very much on his side it was going to be a deadly set of tasks he had lined up for Lena but what she did to make this not possible would be truly extraordinary.

Francesco had a list of missions that he set about Lena doing whilst he was taken away by the police for questioning the first one was to kill her friends.

"No, never to make me do something like that is not me," insisted Lena. "You shall never eliminate us from you were a part of you we love" demanded the inner spirits "impossible i through Francesco the human did" spoke a confused Lena.

Lena walked over and picked up several bits of wood that had a human underneath it the first one she picked up had a very young child underneath it she scowled around the room and saw a crying pair of eyes pressed against the window it was hard to comprehend. She too had floods of tears streaming down her face there was quite major injuries to herself she had to be rushed to hospital urgently. The sounds of sirens came past with speed but went straight past "leave her" urged Francesco "you fucking what?" Cried Lena "you're mental" she dashed out with her high heels in white and tracked it down before it could speed of too far she took her left foot and stuck it underneath a very fast blue flashing light ambulance he slowed down and the people inside took a look in the mirror to see what could be happening they saw a foot wedged underneath. They came to a quick stop and found she had a young children in her hands cradling it with significantly grave injuries. They had stopped with urgency here foot got wedged Francesco's inner spirits were pushing her foot further in by this point the children was still in her hands.

The ambulance crew were scrambled to the attention of they both reacted fast by both working as a team. Duncan one of the crew tried to gently move the ambulance but it was in deeper than she thought the two wheels she had it stuck under where very big and she could feel her feet crumbling but there weren't hurting at all which was very unusual due to the type of situation she was in. she had baby Ann in her hands Lena gave them baby Ann to the doctors with sweat and blood running down her face looking down at her whilst she tried to pull herself out. Although she had got her foot with ease and super speedy she flew back up but she started to fly and processed the eyes of Francesco. Baby Ann was being escorted by the ambulance crew Doug and Duncan in to the yellow ambulance. Baby Ann awoke and started to gurgle one eye opened and she began to cry as she struggled to maintain breath the doctors worked mega fast. Lena was up in the air by this point in a very light blue sky turning rapidly darker. Francesco had arrived at the police station when he changed faces and so did Lena we can't forget of course they are both connected in the way they think. Lena turned back Francesco did the same whenever something in Lena the same happened in Francesco and vice versa.

As the police car drove Francesco sitting in the back managed to disappear within any noise present he was a silent as nothing you had seen before. He was in the sky with Lena they fought Francesco viewed Lena whilst Lena viewed Francesco, "You're the same as fucking me how is this possible," asked Francesco Lena turned her face around and starting heading in the direction of the floor where she had just escorted the young girl to safety she played out the image and recreated once one she showed Francesco the image, followed by a number of other flashbacks that might jog his memory.

Francesco started intendly at them and then back at Lena who was still in the opposite direction, Francesco turned her face with force to get her attention. "That doesn't merit a kiss in my books why are you so violent!" yelled Lena fiercely moments after this happening she turned once again and she never said another word on the subject. She recreated the image in her head and the same ambulance appeared about 50 feet below she went down but before she could do that Francesco the real one had a firm grip and pulled her back

Francesco succeeded back to a nearby lake about a few feet from the scene she got back the grip she needed. Francesco still went after here like there was something was on her that he liked a particular scent? Or smell? In fact to not tell lies she had every smell of Francesco hence why we think he followed. She had gone way into the distance and was down seeing to her emergency as it was before she left, She had still got her leg trapped underneath but for longer this time so Duncan could rescue her and save the day and release her leg. He was successful after about 15 minutes but for baby Anne time was almost up just by seconds. Through seeing this it was vital and critical to come up with a option that would make sure she got the attention she needed the closest hospital was about 15 miles away she wasn't going to make it ½ a minute remained. Francesco struggled to find her trees blocked his way although the trail of Lena's scent was smelt so he knew he was closer than ever before.

The trees swayed from a gust of unknown source of wind it was July 1977 by this point it definitely seemed not quite right but nothing was unusual in 1977. Francesco cut down the trees quicker than you could say Francesco being the quick guy to intervene he would leave no page unturned in the love he had for Lena, All he had to do was keep her under his control for as long as he could if she wriggled out he would have ways to draw her back in keeping her eyes that pale red that was so lovable. He cut through every tree looked behind every nook and cranny every tree he went to the back of to search came to no result leaving him to rapidly fly with time on his side he was able to thoroughly search each and every in sight tree. He was in luck there was a very indulging strong scent of bread with margarine from behind the 20th tree he looked behind. He distinctively knew that that was Lena's favourite with a jam pot ready to spread funnily enough she was doing behind the tree on the silver moon light concrete pavement that lie about 60 feet down from the tree that she was hidden behind. He swooped down and took hold only for a split second Lena's hand. Lena was there knowingly ready for Francesco's appearance, she turned around once again and pushed Francesco back up near his cloud.

Lena won again with Francesco inside of her anything was possible she could Francesco the real one out of her mind at any time she pleased. This was a golden moment to get him out of existence. After all that had happened Lena feel in love with another boy and kept this very much secret from him. His very dark streak of hair went back as far as the trees it was like a bouncy castle. Lena enjoyed this very much and took a lot of pride in being able to manipulate Francesco just like he did to her. Three of her friends turned up by this time Francesco had it coming for him but Lena also changed faces they were lots alike as you can tell.

Chapter 18

FRANCESCO TAKES REVENGE ON LENA

Francesco was still bouncing about and with the help of Camilla, Fleur, and Beatrice it was three against one. Lena (Francesco) through the real Francesco was being sucked all of his thoughts of Lena out of him, there was even a memory of when they were young the memory showed when they were 5 or 6 years old and they both admired each other and the blue eye meet the red eyed Francesco who didn't have any distinct connection with Lena back then was at least the other side of the room to each other the space was hard to watch because you knew very well that there was a connection. they would spent lunches together, breaks, sharing a snack that they both liked it was red in colour and very creamy vanilla tasting it wasn't just them who liked this indulgent treat but everyone else tried to grab one. They wanted to bring a lot as they were a sharing group of people.

People who didn't like to see others hurt but then the other contradicts this very idea by a lot one school day Francesco exited the school life without being told. You're probably how could someone be so sly and sneaky leave without being seen. Despite this he left a very big smell of limes he had a lime jacket on made out of Limes itself he walked into the forest with that smell lingering behind him the forest was so close by that if anyone tried to enter it the teacher would see but this is the way that he was so unnoticeable there was a group that lived in the forest in his one imaginary mind sense he believed that there was something lying in the field more than your average Joe or group of friends that will change you into being something a little bit more controlling a little bit more I will get what I want through doing this and this. Whilst he was in the greenery he wasn't just taken in and changed by a group of students who wanted to give him another angle on the way that he should approach things.

Perseficic subjects were discussed during their time in the maze of a forest plan going forward evil and cunning plans some of these were wicked. As time went on it got darker he had what he wanted looking him in the eyes as he bypassed the corridors or whilst he was in class he would spot Lena at least once or twice everyday whilst he was in the class. They shared Art, drama together just to name a few. They were incredibly creative hence why they got amazing careers further down the line. She continued to produce very quick memories from her bank of memories they were limitless. Her next memory explained what had happened in the story next it was a little complicated to say the least but she would soon go on to explain the reasoning behind this. It went a little something like this when she turned 18 she kissed Francesco down the back alley after going nightclubbing on a night out. They had a group of friends around them and got drunk it was nearing Christmas and one thing led to another thing and a kiss turned into many when she reached 20 and turned up her love by one notch they couldn't hold it in they were so in love. After that they spent the next 10 years together with her mind being taken over by Francesco lots during the 10 years happened. They stayed in each other's arms after 5 years of them 10 they had a child but didn't decide to keep it. This memory had made both of them cry "what you fucking cry about baby" she cried for a long time after there were so many more memories that she had picked up from Francesco it picked on a moment when he had always wanted to be a part of a band he wanted to fit in and tried singing. When he tried to sing his words they got mumbled and muffled out by his other class members.

With this in mind shortly afterwards his voice changed automatically through he hadn't done anything to change it he had something that happened inside of him to get one on the students. He wore suit like attire but without a tie but with a bow tie and a very beautiful silver pocket square on show his voice tenor went up and done according to his line on the sheet music he was very confident and delivered every time. Lena was very impressed but puzzled all at the same time. Francesco invited Lena on stage to sing and accompany himself she was very nervous but when he started dancing and busted a move like seen at the ball she rushed up on stage to join him. One by one they all got up on stage and started dancing to fun music. The music to make you move it was the 1970s the time of Trex, Village People, pussycat etc, after 30 minutes of flashes from the past Francesco felt it was his turn and rightly so. Francesco picked his mind and convinced Lena what she missed there was a time during their engagement when they were married and caring for their little child Theo he ran around and there were connections that Lena made before he was given to someone else.

She took Theo's hand and they went out for lunch, went for a park visit the exact name Lovegreen Park. Lovegreen Park was filled with many children's from all parts of Appleford and beyond outside the city from places such as Bananaville same amount of people lived there as Appleford then you have Chocohaven there was a short footfall of people in Chocohaven. There was precious moments that when the clip ended made her fall on to her knees she had changed back so you know her hands that still felt the warm embrace of his hands it even had the smell of him on him but then she remembered the moment they left each other. Francesco nor Lena had a memory for this it was too painful to reflect on.

After the 10 years were up she had a big decision to make still feeling hurt from the time they had to get rid of little Theo and the sudden departure of Francesco himself she was very keen to continue on with Francesco being ignored so much so she turned around and created a barrier or wall against him and her to accompany this she looked up and made the wind blow faster than it did "You left me bastard" blasted Lena "you asked me to get rid of Theo I loved him" "you didn't keep an eye on him through did you you whore" "slut" the moment Theo had gone at the age of 3 and a half it had been a whole day before the Scottish lass and her sly creepy boyfriend had gone to check on baby Theo, Lena was frantic Francesco showed no sign of missing him in the slightest as she then went on to say "you never missed him dickhead" "it took us a day to release he had gone what kind of parents are we" Confidently spoke Lena hail feel out of the sky during Lena's fit of rage.

The whole of the road was full of colour by this point red yellow pink it spanned back as far as her house. Roxanne left bingo the dog Trevor and everybody else present left to check out the comminution down 62 stretch street the rain was beating against his face the Scottish mountains looked closer at the speed they run they passed every street moving swiftly between them. Whilst back at 62 stretch street they moved themselves further down the street now at 67 stretch street, residents could hear a noise from outside and a police helicopter was back in the skies of Appleford searching every street for the suspects but when they zoomed in on the street number they were given nothing could be seen. Having been aware of the presence of the fuzz in the air they converted to being invisible through all the years they had been on the job PC Tom Harvey coconut and his colleague Sam short for Samantha Lucy spidercuttingworth she had served very loyal to the service her favourite food a big massive juicy burger filled with onion rings and bacon in fact she was consuming one right now whilst using only the state of the art material she knew how they could see what was occurring it's what they were about after all Trevor was running with speed down towards where Lena was located he took had a tracking device which could pinpoint where she was she couldn't hide from daddykins "Oh Lenny" in a very daddy to daughter Lena reappeared but still invisible to the eye in the sky. Trevor looked up and also noticed the eye in the sky remaining out of sight at all times. Trevor would look up and if like there had been some kind of mistake he spun the helicopter upside down with his reverse athon buried deep in his pocket.

Outside his daddy duties you see he was a clown an actor a musician and was Vice President for Appleford and surrounding villages this even included monster village, still in the stages of getting over the loss of Gorgimpus in the previous standoff with Francesco. Trevor had put spiders a fear of Lena's and a trail of bread and jam Lena's favourite for Lena to follow she started to follow but very swiftly remembered that she was competing against the world's powerful power source her dad was very enticing he was to right whilst Francesco was on the left "oh Lennypoo lennypop you know you want to have the bread with jam" said Trevor luring in with puppy dog eyes on the other hand Francesco was still trying to break the metal wall that stand before him and victory. She salivated other the thought of her beloved foods yet Lena was conscious that she had left something reeling she hurried back and continued to tackle Francesco had almost broke through the wall she built she taped it back up generating his cravings he was a big fan of chips and crisps so all of a sudden whilst concealed in a strong taped up piece of the wall you would have you're crisp you would think it be ok to eat it but before you could swallow it fully it would come back out and eat you instead but only a bit of you the size of the crisp shape. He then had a juicy, scrummy piece of pizza come on through to him he stood there as the pizza flew around wanting to be ate he slowly but surely took one bit worried that it might eat him. Eating small pieces was OK it was eating bigger pieces that were going to fall him. To top the icing on the cake she had shielded of the wall to complete darkness acting as a maze for him to figure out with all being monsters.

Lena had devised several uncompleted unforeseen missions from him to undertake. Some of these Francesco had never seen she had the ability to spin Francesco into hers very quickly after all she was very talented and had come from a very talented background. But for how long was she able to get away with it seeing how much of her that he had direct control over from fights past.

Chapter 19

FRANCESCO'S REVENGE PART 2 ON LENA

Lena had left Francesco a maze a very complicated maze of puzzles and riddles to solve it was incredibly dark in the space in the wall he was in. The hole in the wall grew narrower and narrower by the second this time seconds where very compacted together in fact they were so congested it was like cars or sardines. He began to crawl through the first of Lena's mystery encounters all he could hear was a very faint sound of Lena's voice drifting slowly away he could make out Lena going "wooooahhh!!!! I caught him I have my revenge, "Nooo how could this be" echoed Francesco, the smell of jam and bread faded away along with Lena and dad she was she was so badass he thought that he clucked ever so slightly as he moved. He continued to search the tunnel he had before him for clues to an exit. It was incredibly muddy, dimly light and very smelly it was 500 years old this wall. He saw distinctive paintings of what his father use to paint there was a picture of when he was 10 and played football he hadn't seen this in sometime so he peered and observed for about 10 seconds to gain an insight into his life.

The pictures to come going through the ages these were the memories that she never showed him at the time of the breakdown outside of the wall. They were incredibly dusting and sharp to touch as they had been nailed to the wall for some many years. But then it showed his father era. Lena's first clue wasn't to be very far away the space in between him and the first of three continual wins in a row. He started to shake and starting to cough without any stops it could mean danger was around the corner. It became a creaky staircase within that he had to follow they were coloured a red it turned muddy and wet for a time after that. Lena had placed the door so far away that he find it hard to locate it the stars had about 500 to keep him actively fit, he began to miss and gather certain pictures that made him think about the time they were together this tunnel this trap this riddle was made for him to do just that.

About 30 past and the first wall came literally running after him he was getting sucked into it and his face grew in size his body shrunk and his eyes popped. With both of his hands he pushed both of what he could feel where bricks within a metre away from smashing into him. The wall that he was trapped in gave way to a brick that feel on his head this is what Lena had happen to her so had to happen to him. It was like a cave no lights where lite through "Son of a bitch". Lena wanted pay back so here was to that payback happening. A sudden chill a chill much more colder than one care to imagine took full control and blast from the four walls of the tunnel, cave and wall straight to him. Light was seen ahead of him he vowed to himself that he would get revenge and a lot of it when he found an exit. Lena had devised her very own wicked plan. Lena got back skipping and dancing to the fact that she had evolved and got her ultimate revenge and the fact that people would be a lot more safer now that he was gone her house had now been brought back to normal and she had Francesco inside of her so now she could use this to great success and finish were he had left off. Francesco on the other hand was losing his power he had once had and started to fade the power grew weak but he had one way in which he could get back the ruling of his throne back in the sky. He didn't lose sight of his phone his IPhone 6 he had nestled in his pocket. His silver iPhone was indeed in his pocket althrough Lena had throught of this and used whilst he weren't looking she crept into the pocket of Francesco and used all available percentage he had leaving no stone unturned she had a slow moving distract something into thinking hex. This was the darkest but with him away she could take over the headquarters of Francesco cloud in the sky, this was more than 100 per cent powerful he protected it even being stuck he still secured it and monitored its every move that was being made.

He made progressive steps to going through the first trap after going through the pictures and the vast amount of other unsuspecting acts that would trip him up get it lolll that Lena had put in place. There were a few mice on the floor in the direction he was heading in the very direction of them he spotted them very quickly and made a quick dash back but these mice weren't really mice they were Lena's own version of soldiers the ones she saw when Francesco was in control back in the restaurant. In fact talking of restaurants we should see how it's getting on the restaurant was still in the recovery stages the recovery stages consisted of finding the lost, informing next of kin and making certain that the restaurant was back to its old self and ready to eat in and become safe for people to enter. Lena dropped by as a matter of fact past it and meet up with several very close friends who had questions for her "where's that son of bitch Francesco" challenged Camilla, who gave her a massive girlie like hug on meeting and seeing her it was like one of them moments in the films when a reunion happens. It was unique to them. "Well I set about trapping in that wall you know which one I mean right beaut" hinted Lena "I sure do can we see it I want to laugh in that motherfuckers face" giggled Camilla "we sure can baby girl" congratulated Lena.

They both took each other's hands and headed on back to the wall where Francesco was it was about half an hour's walk with Trevor on way back home further than what Lena had been he began searching but spotted that they were safe and she had meet a friend a close dear friend that she had known for 13 years wow, he turned on his feet and went back home. Lena and Cam had reached the wall once again and started shouting "Oh Francesco where are you you know you want to be with me and my gorgeous wife lolll" they both chuckled "I'm looking really beautiful today Francesco I don't think you'd want to miss out on being with me would you" she was true to the word every bit Francesco loved about her, back inside the wall only the faintest of sounds could be heard it was incredibly muffled his ears began to block out any noises as it was early dark and lifeless. Although at this moment the noise started to pick up and Lena and what sounded a lot like Camilla or another close friend of Lena's became present and sounded in his ear drum "Lena is that you i'm so scared right about now help me" he was sweating like a pig by this time it was so dark that he hadn't reach one bit without biting his head once.

There was a riddle that he had to solve before being allowed on to the next bit he had to try and rematch some words back together whilst being under a spell of wanting food and reaching out to it he was aware the faster he acted the quicker he could have the pizza and chips with beans the other side the temptation became greater and greater and greater and greater every passing second he tried to piece the puzzle when all of sudden he could smell something behind him that would make him rush to get the food the fire hadn't reached his legs but was close to doing so. The riddle was to name every member of Lena's family and couple of other questions chucked in for good measure his feet were killing him and the exact same time he became stuck it was quick sand there were two reasons to be quick now. He swore one of his men from the clouds to come and rescue him and one to set up an immediate for Lena still invisible of course. Francesco connected to his cloud by radio signalling through his microphone device only one man was there guarding it.

Once it reached Lena's ears she couldn't believe it "oh shit" she had a whole array of different outfits that would pick from especially in times like this one it called for it. She started to change in a nearby clothing room within 5 minutes she was done "wow that was quick you go gal" chanted Camilla within an inch of Lena at this time. "I'll back very soon wait for me" "take me with you" "of course" Lena had changed her mind fast. Camilla took Lena's T-shirt and started to grab on as she travelled up the grip was getting harder and harder to keep a hold of but Lena being Lena would not let her friend let go she produced a fourth hand out of a third and fourth if that makes sense one came before enough did we mention that she connect 2 hands lolll making 1. She took her 3rd and 4th hand and put it behind her gesturing for Camilla to take them she was scared but knew she was doing for her safety and she flew further up. The clouds done below one earth because what they could imagine was earth. Earth became quickly apparent but it was not where Lena was heading. Now we know what you're thinking who's done below looking after and monitoring Francesco Lena had this sorted she recruited a standby just in case of any absences to herself. Francesco lived not too far away from ground level. As soon as she reached the top through sat nav, she got straight to work on finding where he was talking to his accompanies from. It was steady getting darker on his cloud and the more you were on it the darker it would get. The colours on the cloud changed very frequently to suggest that someone was nearby this is exactly correct whenever it changed colour of sidekicks would be one step closer to finding you.

They found themselves in a puzzle several puzzles just as Francesco was in. Lena placed one foot gently on to the cloud that have several systems that would alert the sidekicks the baddies to your whereabouts. Each was coded so Frank B was orange, Joseph D was purple, Harry F was silver and Scarlet G was green, now for this to take effect fully you had to make sure that you were on the right cloud at the wrong time. The colours weren't always visible to see as it would be a very pale white for a long period of time. Lena struggled her way through the first set of clouds with Camilla racing through them knowing what sequence to do them in, after 20 minutes Lena had gained considerable speed and really got the hang of it she had a sensor that allowed to see what danger was ahead so for instance she saw purple knowing that this was Joseph she took it to extreme lengths to make sure that she placed her foot right across to be able to see where he might be next, Camilla took one wrong step and ended up stepping across and be sucked into the bit of the cloud that belonged to Harry F it was as silver as a knight she never saw anything as silver. Down before on the floor the bodyguard under the ruling of Lena took his job incredibly seriously and guarded the area so that Francesco couldn't escape. In the wall he had to find air and fast as it didn't have very many areas where it was possible to get air he punched one bit of the wall but noticed it had the strongest tape again under the ruling of Lena. He continued on with the riddle as the fiery inferno increased and came closer and closer to him. It came to him he had seen Lena's family before and had remembered asking all their names. He entered everything he could remember. Every name that came to mind Frankie came to mind. The computer had 3 chances connected to it he had to get it right, something beginning with R rowanne, Roxanne he typed in and it went a dark green to tell he had succeeded. He know had to remember the other family members, he pictured the time when he had meet them and asking their names what they could of been, travis, he started typing a blood red colour appeared before him his feet where getting hotter and hotter the fiery blaze almost had engulfed him he had 2 or 3 minutes to be able to conquer the riddle the wall that lie between him and the next level level 2 will he make it? Let's find out

Chapter 20

FRANCESCO'S REVENGE ON LENA PART 3

Francesco spoke everything he had on his mind on to the wall the riddle the computer then bingo hey presto it came to him like a stroke of luck, Trevor, he had one more bit left to go it was split into 3 bits "What is Lena's brothers and sister called" he could feel the fire begin to warm the back of his neck by this point he didn't know another stroke of luck was needed he consulted every bit of knowledge he had stored inside his head. He looked for information to help him, back on the clouds Lena had literally just caught out and was back to the first square on the cloud. She had a brief moment of hesitation and took

2 steps instead of one square being one of the baddies part of the cloud this one belonged to Scarlet G a green colour. All four of them had sprung out waiting to slip up Lena and Camilla they sprung up in multiple parts of the cloud at any one time "here I am" called one. Lena leapt to grab what she uncovered to be the crown Jewel the walkie talkie coloured silver and black not your normal black, his watch that had Lena's face on it and all around watch on what she was doing and his Ring that was coloured the same as her hair so wherever the hair was he could then bounce of his cloud and compose a trap he loved her hair even when they were married and basically had a part of her hair attached to the watch.

Camila turned around and releasing Lena was in trouble came to the immediate action of her friend "I have to get that ring and all other bits he has of me" as they run towards getting the objects back she felt something turn beneath her legs. The cloud had made a turn towards the baddies on the other side of them the baddies where now after them. They formed two separate teams 2 on 2 they charged after Lena and Camilla with no word said there were true amounts believable amounts of violence occurring right about now. Seeing as Lena had the skills that she did processes you'd think that she be able to fit these demons, the trolls the monsters as she would see them as but Francesco before he had left he through a series of drills as Frantastic training HQ (headquarters). He taught them how to if they ever came against the likes of Lena how to be prepared.

During their marriage Lena had used a string of spells that he wouldn't be in the know about. She would so much in disguise be ready to plot her next sinister move against Francesco by using what she had given to her whilst he was building his very own step by step ideas on a bit of chalk white paper he had as far away from her as possible so some time in the not so distant future he could be the one to seek vengeance in defiance of

Lena. Lena was not to be beaten as many a wild beast came for the right so did a raging bull came from the left, in very slow motion she came at the first two baddies it was like a dull moment. You could see Joseph and Scarlett going down first she had upped the ante by this point she went straight through them with finesse, amaziness, flair, expertise she had just before had a very in depth chat with her very own friend standing very close in fact hand to hand they cuddled up and starting talking about three options that were open to them.

They came to striking her first charge forwards, her 4th hand and 1st hand where a success you see her fourth and first finger turned into bigger nails they were so sharp that the impact they left changed the game altogether he turned out Harry this is had took out a several piece missing Jigsaw puzzle. Lena's face started to feel her facial bits come off and as this happened the puzzle started to gain speed and rushed over to collect the bits of the nose this was one of several items that were coming of her eyes were about to fall as well. As this was happening she pulled out a little special something that would get him Harry nervous this thing she pulled out was a helmet but not just any type of helmet it could retract and force back any item that was being taken away from her. Her handbag which she brought with her anywhere she went could also fly it was you're turquoise green colour. So anything she requested all she have to do was just ask and the bag would have it ready. The bag also had the ability to fight back whenever Lena was getting hurt it had eyes and had a visual effects systems it could turn Lena's art that she drew at home into the hands of professionals allowing it to be posted in galleries. It had ears to allow it hear what people were saying and if it didn't like what it heard it moved forward to the attack the individual.

Lena whilst Harry and the other baddy looked shell-shocked also had the ability to bring or force down something from the sky from her very arm all she need do is activate the coding on her arm and call what she could already see from the sky whatever object took her liking she went for she took it out of the sky, she threw towards Harry who allowed it to skim past his head. She needed something harder and with a lot more force. Taking these precious moments would invite Harry to throw some of his objects he had for example he had a slug which has extendable feet and didn't stop growing his feet would get trapped in her eye sockets forcing the opponent not to see out of one or both his eyes. He flung one like you would a tennis ball. Lena looked up and took immediate as this two full over her head but didn't as 5 more were thrown and hit Camilla in the eye "take cover" shrieked Lena as he continued. She had a massive book full of ideas she could use all with the names of different people and what you could do all she need do now is use of them. One suggestion she liked a lot it consisted of the following she took several hair clips, a hair band all out of her hair mixed with a loving scent but this was a set up because it wasn't really perfume it was powder that would go up your nose and cause a itchy feeling in your throat it was powerful stuff in being distracted the hair pin, hair band can get to work with putting it around real tight so he doesn't know what has just happened causing him to faint on the floor.

She came out behind her very own from home set of stairs she had. These were the same colour as her prom night stairs she saw that talked. They had a little pouch bit where you could shelter again at the call of the handbag. She comes out and puts what's in the book into action. What happens next is so glorious and so eye-catching takes your breath believe me it all just flashed past Lena's eyes which were firmly back in place slotted in another you are going to believe this one there not the right way round lolol. She touched them and all of sudden admired the scenery which didn't match what she saw if she looked to the left of her luckily she had a way of fixing such dilemmas ask her friends if she could use Camilla straighten your eyes kit which fixed it in a jiffy Her eyes were altered by the point of Camilla's face turning around "That's a lot better" pointed out Camilla, the hairpin waddled along bashing into the headband quite a bit. It was a race to see who could get there first the headband or the hair pin they were metres apart from each other because they reached the toe as Harry and Joe were getting blasted. Lena had eyes on the prize as she watched from both eyes the way this worker is that all parts of her body could sense from the back and behind. The eye jumped for her eye socket once again and took on to her shoulder and saw what looked like two men charging for her at the back where her spin was located.

After being informed of such things she was quick to move in fact she ran it she had the speed of lion she definitely topped 60 with this super speed she had all she would be required to do is start running and her running speed would increase a lot. The two men behind two built up their speed. But there was something that Scarlet, Harry, Frank and Joseph all didn't know she could lead around in one big circle. As she circled they got incredibly dizzy or started to she took them in one big circle about 50 times it was quite a bit for them to handle and she never got out of breath. As all of them tried to save each other one after the other feel on to each other. But cheeky Lena wasn't going to stop there to try to trick these guys into luring her onto their side.

They were two worlds apart from each other as of present they were on a beach where they had made a very swift shifting to after they didn't think the cloud was a big enough space from them to fight against each other. In an earlier on bit they feel but they didn't want to tell you this they wanted you to think they were still fighting on the clouds. Before they entered the beach they had several obstacles in their path. Francesco devised he have more than more cloud to allocate and position his soldiers on so he had built several more but he wanted to make sure also that they were protected so you had to devise a code to get in which he knew deep inside his pocket also he had silver and golden coins and a set of numbers just like Francesco did down below whilst stuck in the wall although the difference being that the keys were with him and Lena had placed the keys in the wall on the 3rd puzzle. Checking back in with Francesco he had found out how to open the gate there placed a piece of Lena in a puzzle underneath his feet he opened the door with very shaky smelly stinky hands that tasted like mud.

The fiery inferno took two steps back and was forced back by the door. Francesco was on the second puzzle right about now and Lena had raised her game she now put snakes in the entrance of the 2nd maze, monsters, real ghosts without the covers, and bulging eyes, more screenshots of her life with Francesco it was becoming darker and darker every minute he was in a dream he thought in this round the monsters where voices inside the concerted insides of the wall, waiting to bounce to scare you out of your mind with had bulge mc bulge eyes, pizza ghost, crisp head, lightingskull brain, chilli-screamer monster and Ice-cream-melter monster. He couldn't help but want to crease at the thought of this he went in and escorted his eyes around and laughed and was then in fits of it on the floor.

Then voices came from the walls of the wall itself several notes could be read which she left "have fun I know you'll love the names that I have come up with" there was a switch next door to the note he switched and the first ghost made its appearance it was crisp all covered with every type of crisp imaginable first of all to make him really hungry he cast a long ranged spell which looked red a red line appeared and through putting both hands to his temple and started massacring it to create this whirlpool of red all you could see from the outside was a bloody red colour which if you came close would also make you hungry and cause you to tell your friends by which point you would be in there to with Francesco the red colour became more and more as crisp head summoned all available strength and power from him to become hungrier. His body began to make noises telling him he was hungry crisps were hurdling towards him each flavour made his nose and his stomach want it he even got up and grabbed one of them to it flying away each flavour he loved and any flavour he loved his predecessor Lena would to.

A waft of salt and vinegar came up to the noise of Lena going through her nostrils and lighting up her taste buds. The crisps piled up it was filling up fast the wall expanded and was close to exploding with crisps he couldn't stop eating his body was still having urges he climbed up the ladder of goodness and jumped in having lots of fun he never gained a pound. Back to the beach where Lena was she had managed to fight her way through the men very successfully without any problems, it was a particularly violent brawl if I do say myself they did use a lot of comebacks to try and gain back control but didn't win as after half an a hour she'd feel a lot injuries that healed very smoothly and very efficiently. She did a very made up victory dance to follow but then one got up once more and managed to rebuild as well he'd changed back to Francesco? How could this be possible? His face matched here's when she looked like Francesco but she had turned into a female version of him. She laughed in constant amounts he had lip stick in his right hand with a mirror in the left. She or he however you look at it whichever angle you take it from.

She or he screamed loudly and fainted afterwards she pulled out of her talking purse within her bag a large heroic banner for times like this it said "Lena rules motherfuckers" she created this at school and brought it home Roxanne invited her to put up on the wall they went like school girls up the stairs and came dashing through the door like excitable puppies they had put many an achievement of Lena's up on the wall. She couldn't of been more prouder there eyes circled the room like owls eager to share her successes she had ran down the spiral stairs they had on that afternoon of April 15 1974 after completing an art project prior to coming home and flung her arched windows to her porch and had a lazy afternoon in the sunshine they lived in a mansion Trevor didn't want any less. She went down also on that afternoon to allocate a deckchair to sit on and soak up the rays she rummaged through the high piles of antics she didn't already know she had. There was everything from chess that had cobwebs to quite a lot of dust she took it out and unearthed a guide on how to play it and pieces from the set she was a little rusty back then but she couldn't but want to stand there and bask in the history of the family.

Right next door she found a doll which was here's she still to this very day has a lot of toys that she keeps memories of but this doll was a lot older. Trevor had once told her a story at her beside and handed over a very pricey position she went to hug it and even to this day she broke down and shed a tear or two. She removed it from the shed where when Lena showed Trevor what he had found couldn't want to get it fixed up and patched up ready for Lena to use. Inside of Mazda X8 boot lie a while collection of creative tools he could use. Lena was immensely proud and hugged her dad tight and called out to him "I love you daddy" he replied with "I love you too" the joyous moments stayed with her and know when she looks into her car a Ford Fiesta the very precious moments return back. Lena still reignites with her dad to relive that very day even now. This was not the only set of baddies Francesco had in mind the later she got down the clouds it was banned levels 1-5 of difficulty but she knew she could beat them but they're super crafty it intensified by a lot.

Lena had a lot still to learn about these baddies. She thought bring it on one level as they jumped of the cloud on to the next levels that occurred the next one contained someone who spoke French. Francesco was multi-lingual and was constantly reviewing how much he knew and how much he needed to learn. Adalie tested them to the fullest "Bonjour comment-allez vous she began by saying further french came from the genius "Comment vous appelez vous?" "can you tell me what that means to the side of her lie a big clock that she looked up she would refer back to this when she was counting down the minutes they both looked at each other with questioning looks do you know type of looks. Down back on ground level Francesco was still stumbling through Lena's death defying traps. He was coughing out little bit of crisp remains he had in his mouth he had took cover under the crisps to trick crisp head and it worked he searched for him but wasn't able to find him crisp head looked through areas to aid his search in finding gold. In fact it was so sly that you can't describe in words he moved on through the narrow dark dimly light tunnel shaped as the wall he tapped the next button closed to him and found that before he knew it he was greeted by the next monster in line that Lena had set for him Pizza ghost. Pizza ghost the aroma of Pizza's of every topping known to man available this time he didn't have the one crisp head made an appearance he through his sonic vision he had tracked where he was and on this occasion there was no way he was going anywhere. You can see from one side there was a gate barricaded and what was going to happen if he didn't follow what was being asked of crisp head and the other side there was this massive variety of crisp heads there now stand before him a yellow crisphead shaped just like a crisp then you had a head shaped as the pot you get you're vinegar out of he went to the floor in fits of laughter. As he was laughing crisp head homed in on him and one crisp flung out of his hands and spent very little releasing it from his hands his hand flicked it towards Francesco hitting him on his eyelid he put his right hand on his eye like he knew and took it off and began eating familiarising himself with the flavour his taste buds lite up with flavour he didn't know but he was going to fall into the same trap as he done before.

Back up in the clouds Lena was prevailing all the way through she was a genius there could be no ifs or buts or no denying such things she had it and Francesco was losing it was like she would go and increase her ways of celebrating she did some great stuff trust me. That was pretty much it Lena had found what she needed after Francesco's version of an army came out at Lena. There was everything from soldiers to very luxurious food items that were admittedly so tantalising great in every way it was hard but of course with her friend close by every minute of the adventure she had made it possible. Darker times were still admittingly around the corner and it wasn't over but she could say that she had gone through at least 5 rounds of Francesco known madness. Down below with Francesco he knew one thing for certain that crisp head had a strong grip on and he no plan on getting off. He chucked the same thing and he fell under the spell he lay talking about crisps crisp where in his every thought when he opened his sticky eyes where the crisp had caught it and the crisp had the grease which allowed to stick pretty hard. He tried opening them and had considerable difficulty whilst doing it. He continuously tried to open his eyes and after 10-15 minutes of trying he is very triumphant in doing so he starts throwing what he would use in defence something called franks balls lolol get it they're spicy and you shouldn't of seen their eyes the outer bit of the ghosts eyes lit up red following this he did a muffled scream that became noticeably not heard this was incredibly odd he lay a foot or two away from the ghost lunging at him. He wasn't wrong he swooped in and started to wrestle with Francesco to get him to the ground and make a blow at him. In the first swoop he didn't failure he got Francesco and when Francesco awoke all he could visibly see is the inside of the ghost very transparent very different very unique to all other insides of any human or animal's body. Francesco made progressive steps to get out but the ghost had thought about this one and had lots of defences with everything to fences, to gates to vomit slides, to make him go back down again but we all know Francesco he will get out let's find out.

Chapter 21

A GHOSTLY TRAP FOR FRANCESCO

Francesco made many attempts to find clues to get himself out there was several things that we're putting into place he created several ways of his own to get out also he was close with one of his ways/contraptions but fell before he got to the top his first foot and then second followed he ended up in the exact same place as he started the gooey green funnel he fell from what felt underneath him like ghostly skin but changed into a very bumpy tunnel ride full of leading to the very pit of his stomach you could see specks of light indicating the opening to his stomach but before he could get there he heard several voices speak out to him these were voices he knew but he couldn't fell them and couldn't touch them. The voices got louder and wanting he tried to dodge every corner he could to get an idea of where they were his stomach turned and he became increasingly slow as he was growing in fear the pain had caught up to him and a sickly urge came about him almost feeling the urge to be sick he tried to move faster and not have regular recurring thoughts. His whole body recreated images time and time again. He knew he wanted to reach the voices but the images created in his mind slowed him down. He started to vomit the picture that Francesco had formulated in his head starting floating out of his head and he could soon see it with his very eyes it showed him a lot list of possibilities of who it could be behind down at the end of the tunnel leading to crisphead's stomach. It was a mindmap drawn up by his own mind. He took a smell at him with his vomit filled hands and it smelt like parchment only a lot more so if that makes sense. Then he saw two black shadowy shapes appear from where the tunnel curved around and went around to form the next part. They started shouting his name "Francesco" "Francesco" Francesco felt something pull at his stomach and mind as he produced this black figure like he had just given birth or somebody.

Francesco's name got called again and after slow progression he got to the part where they were calling him at with no one there. The black figures where a lot children as they would mirror everything a child would do. They held Francesco and she could see once again Lena in there future form. He tried to fully register this in his head as to how such things could of made him remember things like this. The figures guided him in a very different route than what was first expected. It was incredibly narrow as he crawled he saw what they called his special place that they made when they found each other again. It was a tree but inside of it lie little messages that they use to send each other in secret some of their darkest ones. Francesco saw very little of Lena up in this very tree when they came home from school only on particular days of the week was she allowed to see Francesco. They had names for each other Frankie or Lenny that type of thing. Francesco had came with the suggestion of using his craft tools he had located in his house underneath his bed to piece together a box to share all their secrets all those moments they spent together and put under this tree. Francesco formed a massive big smile.

Crisphead from the outside knew that he had to see what was going on he had this hunch a feeling that something was going on inside him something that would be of help to Francesco he took one ghostly hand and put a glove over it because he didn't like to get wet or messy he had a list of his dos and don'ts. The figures were aware of a hand coming towards them if you turned around from the leafy green tree oozing out real good vibes you could see several cams monitoring the outside movements of the ghost crispy. Crisphead had one of his hand making its way down his throat to find and search for them he had even put little crisp figures attached for good measure. They were close, speedy and very fast all black figures like human shadows barricaded all areas to gain access via they were keen to spend time Francesco sitting him down bringing him back and making sure he didn't come to harm. All areas where tightly secured to disallow little crisp head to appear. The black shadows shaped as human had many a surprise for Francesco, he sat with both feet crossed sitting up-right very pale with a hint of pink in his face with his hair ruffled. He was given a photo that was given to Lena by him way back in there 4th year the picture sucked him in allowing his mind to wonder. He really wanted it to be different this time all of it was how it should've been the way it was told in the picture completely missed out what it was really like but if you took a picture surely you would think it be correct then Franky looked again and released a missing part of the picture that had been taken out.

Franky stepped across the grass in the photo which was more greener than on previous occasions it looked fresh and smelt very fresh as well there had for sure a lawnmower over it you couldn't fault it. He goes over to the garage and sees more than car present he feels inside his pockets and feels keys to suggest someone drove he was truly puzzled. Lena called from the window with her hair coming towards the floor she opens her window very slowly as to of known who it was that could be around the corner she even voices who she thinks it is "Franky" he stood by the window and Lena blew a kiss which came towards his forehead and formed many more and then she chucked down with love that Lena kissed beforehand a card it was big he opened it and is greeted by a picture of them two. Before he came around she had visited her local card shop and got him the only best but didn't need to put anything on it because when she was at home it was all from the heart of her home. She came down a nearby chimney which became very rickety during her climb down Lena was close to falling but whilst she was falling she had just enough time to see how caused her chimney to become unsteady it was Francesco but then through the space of seconds he caught her in a time of need he was desperate to he had changed from his original state he was in moments ago to a transformed man, Lena following this went back up and was keen to find out a little bit more on the type of person that Francesco, she looked around her room for any evidence that might suggest what Francesco was and why he might be changing. She ran to the library it was about just after 9 ock shortly after the gesture was made and Francesco had offered a hand to Lena. Lena knew she had to find out more and she knew by going to the library it would help. There first scheduled date was going to be in this house where Lena fell from.

Lena arrived back to look out the rusty cobwebbed window to find him gone. She began searching for him she raced down the stairs but stumped upon one because she wore high-heels. She very quickly got back up without feeling any side effects from it. She examined her knee and found not a cut on it. She walked around the house and it would only be right to think that her mum had gone she wasn't there. She made herself tea before she went out. The book she got whilst in the library really did match him she had run her finger down until she stumbled across a picture of him. He as she wasn't aware of yet didn't know that when having a look at the book with his face on that he was a great painter, actor and author of his own and he portrayed this by drawing as well. She spent many hours reading through the book with the painting of him on it entitled the greatest work of Frankie D. This is the name that most people called him before he switched to Francesco. He had commonly used this in college a lot.

Lena headed on out and left no stone untouched whilst looking for the man the myth the legend. Deep down there was a burning desire of love for him. She walked along and passed a very familiar identical looking park, the way she knew this was that when she looked down at her feet the paths became like a hill exactly the one she goes up to this very day. Lena climbed up the 20 mile trek to the park as she had also down as a very young child and entered through the gates to the park it was becoming dark and this park had a history of having very interesting unsuspecting creatures come up after dark everything had been sighted even in the newspaper there were regular stories that addressed this. Lena wasn't scared of any ghosts or any creatures she walked in and scowled the park. As she got towards a tree or what looked like a tree the first animal or creature made its appearance. Lena froze for a second then tried to connect with it was very huge. The alarming look in her was intense but she stuck by her word. She started to feel a uncontrollable urge to cry she dabbed her eyes very quickly as to not looked embarrassed. "Fuck" she whispered the tears were continuous. Something then crept up behind her and started dabbing her eyes for her the light up in her face of what she would see next would be incredible. She turned with only one heel to look to see who it could be. Due it being dark it became difficult to see who it was he lunged in for a kiss with both lips connecting for a least 5 minutes. Lena jumped in and put her arms around him. Francesco from looking at the picture for 3 and a half hours after looking at his watch which showed time very differently with the 12 in a different place on the watch and other scattered numbers seemed to remember him being the one who was looking for Lena too after he ran away he wanted to be back in the arms of Lena soon after he left. He quickly reached out and put both arms around her to. But it was still a mystery as to who was the figure hugging her she could only go by who she had in mind at the time. Then he came forward the face came very visible and then it became clear Francesco had returned Francesco took Lena's right hand and lifted it up and kissed it he also rubbed his head against her hand and Lena followed on without another question.

Lena had got home with her love as they were heading home a bridge came into view. Francesco did not for a couple of minutes notice that his hand was being held until he reached out and didn't feel anyone there he begun to get very worried then he spotted the very bridge they spoke about only a few second prior and then released where she was he ran so fast that you thought he was late for a meeting. Lena was posing next to bridge with wide open hands the bridge had lite up with both their names. His jaw dropped she had gone to do this just for him he went closer to the bridge and there was certainly more than first meet the eye. The bridge was covered with their names on it banners wise. The banners had on them Lena and Francesco forever. Lena stand in between them Francesco moved forward and put his left hand around Lena and she followed suite. They both looked starry-eyed into each other eyes "look Francesco babe I apologise for running away from you but I love you and I wanted to do something to show you that" Francesco dabbed his eyes this time around and then he felt uncontrollable tear urges. Lena had one other surprise for Francesco she produced fireworks for them two set for this time they didn't fail them. "wow this is incredible" stared Francesco into Lena eyes "you're very welcome indeede baby" whispered Lena. "Lena you're my everything my oyster, my rock my everything" before he could finish this heartfelt message extremely cute one to Francesco was silenced.

Moments beforehand you could see Lena anticipated what he was going to say because she immediately started to blush and happy tears rolled down her face. The Scottish lass knew what she wanted after the speech they locked lips again as the fireworks and banners where flying high it was a magical moment. Lena head was placed on Francesco's shoulder as they continued a very joyous occasion they had hands in each other's then out of nowhere Lena felt her hand get bigger it got very big it was something very big and had a very lovely fragrance drifting off it. Lena chuckled and had the biggest smile beaming from her face he revealed a very beautiful set of flowers that he picked for earlier on. Francesco's proudest moment as he recalled every moment from observing the picture he could even name the flowers he looked around aimlessly for answers they shrugged. Francesco didn't mind he took a very photo if the day as he kept a photo album of every he had done. Francesco put his head in his hands why did he not continue on with Lena?. "I am the biggest fool" voices spoke around him and comforted him "it doesn't have to be over you can still get her back you just have to find your demons" demanding the figures he opened the book once more and took out the picture and clutched it to his chest and then placed in his pocket. There was one more copy left in his photo album he placed it in the tree where he would end up storing all his beloved cherished moments at some stage or another. He had to find her this had been one of them moments where it was time for action and lots of it.

Francesco started crawling with very numb legs he shook them off and jumped for joy knowing that he would find her all he have to do is trace back his steps. The diverted route he took had shrunk somehow by about a millimetre he became tightly compacted in with his new friends. All of sudden his foot starts dragging him back he battles with it and continued to move but it is very reluctant to let go so much to do that when he moved one step forward it would dig further into the lining of his foot and cause a very in depth foot injury that he couldn't help but feel was this Lena giving him early warning signs. He fought long and hard and dug his fingers straight into the ground to allow to not take him any further. The entrance came further and further away allowing it to not be in the range of the human eye "what has got me guys" called out Francesco. They all looked around at each other giving blank looks until someone came forward. At first it looked like some sort of angel it had exactly the same coloured wings but brighter. Francesco put his hand above his eyebrows it dazzled him and all of sudden he had gone with the spirit "where you taking me" "Lena" "anybody" said a fearful anxious Francesco. The spirit had took him directly back to where the picture had placed him as he had said he wanted that moment never to end so here was his second chance but who had sent this mystical being.

He had arrived back that time when he was first dating Lena there were a few bits he thought he needed to patch up "you have exactly an hour before you return back best of luck" as the spirit patted him on the back. It was incredibly vital that he do things better this time round he was going to bet these demons of his the angel had granted him an hour to do something incredible. He constructed a set of instructions of how he wanted to do this he was determined courageous and very willing. First and foremost he returned home and rummaged through his wardrobe picking the best suit he had out he tried it on and examined just to make sure he hadn't got it incorrect in any way on this very day that he had been set back into he always had several treats coming his way something the picture album didn't go into. He ever so slightly propped open the door after believing he heard a noise the noise grew in pitch and start to be heard from the bedroom. His brother mason had got to the top of the steps crawling and was coming in the very direction of Francesco Frankie for short. Francesco didn't want to make noise unless someone caught him out so he only had socks on. He hid in every possible hiding spot he could find then Pauline his mum and Lucas his dad came up there was no hiding them guys but he looked at his watch and found he only had 40 minutes to patch things up with Lena making this opportunity count. In a frantic attempt to fool his parents. Like a very sly cat he took off into his bedroom and got to work as silently as he possibly could on a manikin doll of himself. He had various arty materials in front of him which he could use to his advantage he went towards the table that he put all his artistic stuff on and rattled through as quickly as he possibly could without disturbing any other known human outside his bedroom or anywhere in his town. This never happened he had been super quick all throughout but when he walked back he slipped over his lead for his computer and he came crashing down causing someone to have second thoughts about checking upstairs it would happen to each Pauline who would come up and check.

Francesco had saw to hiding many moments she'd even thought about going upstairs. "Francesco darling I know you're up here" chuckled an amused Pauline, Pauline had a way of thoroughly searching until she found what she was after. She was in the understanding that he was up here somewhere and his presence was known by all. All you had to see or detect was a console he loved to play on switched on in this case yes, and the controller sprawled out over the floor ready to fall over any minute. She happened to spot this a short time after she flung open his door into his bedroom. He became red faced because mums have that knack to know where you are and they don't stop till they find yer, Francesco crawled slowly from his hiding place whilst Pauline's back was turned and cleverly pulled it off. Pauline looked under his very tidy bed for him and didn't quite spot him. Although was she did notice when she went underneath was a little present that was left for him and a note the note read Dear Pauline, I wanted to let you know i love you very much and thought I'd give you a present after the passing of grandad this year I hope you're OK I'm here if you need me and need to talk by the way I'm seeing

Lena, my girlfriend from school Ps: you're going to love the present yours Francesco, she read the note and felt loved.

Pauline knew that Francesco had always loved her but up till now didn't know this much if you get what I mean if that makes sense. His way of writing always had her wanting to give something to Francesco, but he had U.K. found so the plan she had in mind was to make this plan known she tiptoed in her own little way towards the lights turned them on and couldn't help but say "you got me Franiepoo" her nickname for him but I saw what you got me underneath your bed and I can't help but want to love you and kiss you" he was taken aback he had to come out hearing this he couldn't leave his mum on tender hooks he emerged from his hiding place his hiding place under the blankets of his mom's bed. They both called at each other with no luck to start off with but then she came out at the exact same time as he did they had banged into each other with Pauline suffering the biggest blow she fell unconscious with a huge cut on her head. Francesco kneeled down and assessed the immediate damage he pushed her hair away from the cut and found blood in her hair. The blow to her head would leave wanting to be out for some weeks.

Francesco visited Pauline in hospital a short few weeks after that when he had pulled back her hair he indetenificed that he had gone to considerable lengths to make sure that he had done everyone in his power to make the cut seem less bloody and less intense than it originally was. Pauline had made a very quick recovery thanks to this gesture of Francesco's that night.

Francesco was pacing along the hospital bed before she awoke. Francesco ran over to the hospital bed to immediately hold her hand. She sat upright and tried to recall the events of that night a week ago. She began talking but as she did something didn't quite look right her mouth didn't look right as she was producing the words. Francesco noticing this ran for a doctor. When they returned he had stated that it was very normal to see this happen. He hadn't slept so the picture in his mind the doctor said would look slightly "you should rest m'boy" the doctor said placing his hand around the neck of Francesco. His mission to find Lena was still on track he just wanted to make sure that he cared for his mum and loved her. It was a few days before he exited the hospital with his mum shortly leaving the hospital doors and floors he took 4 steps at a time as he rushed and sprinted down the flight of them. He turned right and was out of sight. He had gone down a very familiar to himself and Lena type of road. The road was muddy and all full of trees they loved going down here to spend some quality time together so if he wanted to replay what he saw in the picture this would be the best place to start and to ultimately find her. He took a far few sharp bends and turns and it all started flooding back to him. In front of him he saw an exact replicate of him talking there time admiring the scenery. He sat down for a few seconds to really smell the hair and sit by their favourite as he sat there he feel his hand being held once again he turned around and Lena had returned stars lit in his eyes he was so happy to see her again and vice versa. They embraced in a hug but what wasn't know where it was real or some sort of illusion playing with his mind he was still incredibly tired and did feel like nodding off. Lena reassured she was real she caught him.

It was 3.30 in the afternoon when he had awoken once more to see Lena carrying him he awoke as Lena peered in to say "Hello sleepy head" gently whispered Lena as through not to startle him or disallow him not to sleep any further he looked like a baby. As Lena would go on to say. Lena lovingly placed her hand on his face and tickled his beard there hands interlocked once more as Lena know what he had been summoned her to do. Lena whisked Francesco back to the scene of the fall but this disallowed him to change. Lena took one leg and flung over the window and then the second leg with Francesco done the bottom ready to catch. To prevent him from failing this time around she put ice breakable ice so that if he didn't catch her which he would then he would fall. It was a second chance he couldn't fail there wasn't any time to fail they were boyfriend and girlfriend it was special "are you ready Francesco" sounded Lena in a commentary tone of voice. She moved at some speed her long ears formed a slide that she could go down she was about 60 seconds from reaching the bottom when Francesco in slow motion runs towards her as she is saved by her beloved Francesco. Francesco had not missed and there they were celebrating and cheering. They heard they're famous romantic play from in the distance and feel instantly back in love. But what caused 10 years to pass with them breaking a fret that? Lena was very keen after this success to keep building on their successes.

One hour was up but this wasn't to be the only memory he need to change. The angel reappeared and was very without delay back in the tunnel this was definitely a starting point. The branches of the tree still had a hold of them as through to say he had missed out something he didn't do on that night. Before he could think about his demons came back and changed the way he viewed that forever. He said words that would mirror what his demons would say and started using everything single that his demons called him to do to get out as soon as he could. He didn't care he blasted the tree branches off with a very strong kicking off his foot his feet were made of the type of stuff that could kick anything that got in his path to exiting something away within seconds he created a fireball from his mouth and chucked in the direction of his protectors his friends the fireball got bigger and bigger and caused them to go very far back. He had erased that from this memory but they had not given up just yet. As he ventured forwards so did they.

He came within seconds of reaching the gate when all of sudden he was struck down and Lena's voice played within his head. All the evil spirits inside him as they would refer to him back as there evil mr, turned Lena's voice into something different and his whole body mouthed again. Spiders, bats and other creepy crawlies begun multiping his hands turned smaller his ears wider his eyes bulged out he had formed wings but there were just one there were two of them then four and then millions. He flew straight past the gates that he passed to gain access to the secret area to now escaping crisp head. But there was one thing he had to do to make sure crisp head man was to become aware that he was exiting he created a noise like Francesco in the body of Crisp head to make him still be in the belief he was still there he had also planted several other death defying noises to falsely-tricking him to wondering whether Francesco was still inside him they all got set off at once as Francesco the now bat had left Crisp heads body he ployed a bomb to go off at any minute as well. Francesco stood well back as millions of varieties of crisps fell into the hands of the needy public it was like raining crisps but better.

Chapter 22

THE FIGHT TO BREAK OUT OF THE WALL

Francesco had been in the wall for three days now with his parents getting incredibly worried. It was all over the news that he had gone. Pauline sit in her seat rocking up and done very quickly. His dad doing the same. As they await news on where he was. He was coughing he was getting incredibly dizzy and had several cuts to the head. The events whilst he was in the wall where fantastic the porches were days away from giving birth to triplets, his youngest had started school and could walk. The town had grown and there had many marriages take place. He missed out on a lot but he fought on let's get a update on what's happening in his world he had defeated crisp head man and had many a crisp to eat and now was coming to attack pizza head his next enemy. But this point the memory had vaguely come back about him and love for Lena. He wasn't clear yet but sooner rather than later he would have to get back after what had been shown it was killing him. He gestured up towards the ceiling of the wall and prayed for her safety and wherever she may be she be something where she was with her family the next ghost was ready to go. He took the first pepperoni pizza and chucked one of many at his face the pizza remains was dripping down his face pepperoni was incredible the smell you couldn't help but want to consume the pizza he started to chew. He always lick at his face it was so yummy that he became preoccupied the pizza ghost tapped him on the shoulder with no response but then he found himself down all eaten up by the pizza ghost. It was the same as the crisp head ghosts body but slightly different you could see the outside of his body and like crisp head he didn't have the power to get rid of him or send anything in to get him. He had different ways of getting into his body but he didn't up go towards the body of the pizza head but he went towards his factory or where the pizza was made on the way there it became dark but then came the pizza factory making process the deliciousness caught up with his noise the delicious taste invited him to go straight in he couldn't leave but as he did this someone had followed him down it was Lena "Francesco you fucking forget me how could you" screamed Lena.

Francesco was still under the influence of his inner demons his evil beings inside him that takes over his brain was still present "Francesco I trusted you" bellowed Lena. Lena moved in for the kill but was also put under the influence of pizza it was so good she ate and ate and ate until she came across Francesco and remembered all she started attacking Francesco with all her might he tried moving but then a repeat of what had happened with crisp head exactly like it said on the tin. Francesco attempted moving but was drawn back in every try the angel returned to show him what was on Lena's mind this time. He was back moments after that very scene near the house there was something truly troubling the school girl back then that he had to get fixed. He got the first bit right but then what happened after that moment was playing with her thoughts.

After that day they returned back to school but only interacted with each other every so often. They bumped into each other quite a lot into each other so much so that they had to talk at some point. There was one point when they were talking they both came out of class at the exact same time. They looked at each other intently for the best part of 10-20 seconds before one spoke "how are you doing" started Francesco "Im great yourself" replied Lena, "how was your lesson?" giving Lena a loving look. "It was quite fantastic" "what did you have" "Oh I had history" "history is one of the best" he leant in for a kiss and got one she put her hands around her and they started kissing however there was something afterwards that didn't match up for Lena. Lena rewinded forward to the end of the day. Francesco had just finished Maths, the last period of the day. When he came out however through Lena was running towards him and ready to kiss and hold hands and spent more time with him. But Francesco walked off and didn't acknowledge she stand there confused and dumbfounded. Francesco had walked past his one and only. He went in a very straight line out of sight. Lena went chasing after him wanting to know more bad questioning his moves.

Lena followed Francesco for a least a couple of miles until she saw him under a tree deep in thought and potentially talking to himself he cried out one name and that was Lena's, Lena went to the third tree and sat by it the tree that Francesco was the other side of and saw engraved writing. The writing was in deep and both of their initials. Francesco head peered from around the tree as he could see Lena looking and observing something "what would you be observing my dearest" gasped Francesco. Lena looked up and pointed one eye in the direction of Francesco "Oh darling I was just looking at the engravings on this tree it is us" she pointed to the tree to signify what she was saying.

Francesco came out of his hiding spot and apologised for his erratic behaviour back over at the exit to the school. He went on to tell Lena about his mission he was sent and said he wanted to tell Lena in a more private place hence why he ignored her she was still puzzled she thought they were going out she had to ask it "I thought you loved me?" She broke down. Francesco felt inside bad and hugged Lena who put her arm around his to show she accepted his apology "we are in this together remember that" as she put hands on his face and we will fight this together. But was this the only thing troubling her. They spent some time devising a plan as to how they were going to go forward to achieve the goal she had a rough idea of how and what could be the thing that he needed to change she had to pinpoint it through. They ventured together further into the forest when the plan was constructed and put together. She took him to the furthest part of the forest where it became dark and you could multicoloured bats flying around you with their pricked up ears and there menacing looks. Francesco paused with Lena going a little ahead and stopping a short time afterwards "have you seen something baby" he had envisioned Lena getting hurt he couldn't allow to be the case and it was going to happen soon. Francesco wanted Lena to stay close.

Whilst back at the school everyone searched entering the area where she was last seen this was Camilla, B, Mike, Nicholas, Frankie and Scott, Scott and his friends went forward one by one hiding behind each other. They had picked through a game of who said someone's name the most goes in first. Frankie was picked after her name was called lots Frankie was the highest in the school and had got the highest grade in maths and English with getting at least a C in both he was in final years and almost ready to graduate he was of big build and had muscles that could pick up people it was incredible how many people he could pick up 2 3 4 even 5. He was popular with girls the girls were around him 24/7 he had currently 4 or 5 girls running after him he found them incredibly attractive and very hot he was dating outside of school hours. They all marched alongside Frankie, within seconds of reaching the forest the group stopped most of them had run off in a scaredy cat type of way. Frankie, Joe and Isabel were the only ones left they moved in and noticed the same tree that Francesco and Lena were sitting under they went up closer to it and saw engravings on with LF and FS "What could they mean?" puzzled Joe, Frankie remembered something Lena always use to tell her if you see anything like this then it's this. She took a double chocolate cookie and a scrap of paper out of her pocket. The note read if you are to find these names this is what it will be for your references. It said Lena franklin and Francesco silk skin. They all didn't not know anything about these being there 2nd names.

She looked around her friends to see if anyone else knew this with all blank faces coming back to her. She looked back at the bit of paper for hints for where to go next. Lena left a note stating where she was likely to go but not mentioning everyone that was up to the team to find out where they could be. They were highly suspicious during school hours they would creep out and go and find something deep within the forest. They were not going to give up at any cost something wasn't quite right about Francesco and Lena had to be warned. She called her "Lena" shouted Frankie, Frankie was her bestie they had been for 10 years all the way through school and college but she knew that she had a thing for Francesco. As they use to sneak out of class a lot and went through to what looked like a forest they would be out of sight before you knew it. Frankie saw footsteps that looked directly like someone she knew through college and school they were Lena's she had the biggest heels anyone could ever have she liked to call them biggies because you could see them imprinting wherever she went she followed them and came across an adorable puppy. Lena was a bigger lover of puppies so she had to be close by. On the other side of the forest about 5 feet away from where they were, Lena and Francesco were laid on the floor spending quality time together. They peered into each other's eyes birds flew around them in and sung. Frankie heard something being incredibly tall she could also look around and see where the noise was coming from. The birds flew up as Frankie then spotted her. But before she could be reached there were several paths Frankie had to track the noise of the birds she picked the 3rd path.

As she trekked down that path she heard eerie noises something had blew her of her feet and had elevated her into the air. She pushed and requested that her friends help. Their mouths fell open at the sight of this. Joe the scientist highest in his class shouted out "it's a skidmick" there the biggest known worms ever in existence here in birchfield. What they weren't aware of is that Francesco planted this a trap to stop them from seeing Lena. The skidmick or skiddy as Francesco liked to call them but a wall out of it's to deter them from coming through. On the other side between the other Frankie and Lena things where getting more loved up and getting more suspicious as Francesco insisted upon moving a little further on down the forest they moved fast as Francesco released he was being followed. They had gone about 2 miles away from the original spot.

Frankie moved followed he continued to go until they were running it was such a precious moment that he didn't want to lose this moment with her that he went to the deepest and darkest depths to do it. Frankie knew though she could be heard even through the sharpest ears. Frankie ran further and further into the forest following the footsteps. Lena grabbed hold of Francesco real tightly as they could. But as Frankie continued to tread through the sticky mud from the previous night's rain as she run her sight became a lot more blurry as a very thick fog descended over Frenzy forest the branches became a distraction and as she run she was close to slipping which she was very close to doing but kept her a very firm grip on the ground. Her facial looked more determined than ever. They held hands and forced their way through with lots of success they had got to the furthest part of the forest. You could look up and the finest blood like rain.the rain turned a very dark purple by this point and started to pierce their skins although for Frankie it went straight through "Lena I'm coming for you" she threw one hand to the air and starred yelling to the air and her feet carried her away very quickly the rain had still caused her considerable setbacks as she "ow" stopped and then did it again. The other guys were on the floor they tried getting up but there face got bigger and exploded.

Frankie looked on turned out her phone and took pics immediately and was crying with laughter. Frankie looked at the sky once more and looked up at a particular object which gave her ideas of where Lena's voice was coming from. Frankie the second enticed in the direction of a old deserted rusty brown house nearby about 2 miles in his direction and in the other she heard Frankie, she had a big decision to make what was she going to do she wanted to spend time with Frankie but did she want to leave her friend. Her hands were tied she looked Frankie in the eye with the impression of wanting to stay on but here friends wanted to find her and reunite and head back to school. She held so tightly on to Francesco hand that is becoming red she made her decision so quickly it was unreal she stayed with Francesco after she fell into a curse a trap of Frankie's that he put on her shortly before she made up her mind. They hurried towards the old crooked house that was draped in history.

As they closer and as Frankie didn't hear any movement of Lena coming forward she begun to get worried and a bit portrayed, Something didn't add up why would Lena not come forward towards her friend. She had a feeling inside that told her not to give up this was coming for mind and the soul. This carried her forwards they reached after about 50 minutes of high blowing winds and not being able to see the way forwards, they saw what looked like Lena's necklace she had left on the floor in a state of hurry. Lena was up ahead but not that far up ahead so much so that her friend made out a shape a lot like Lena's. Frankie the other one Lena's girlfriend ushered her into the house to find that this was where he had his second house he had comfy sofas, colourful pictures and a red carpet like floor for guests like her. She sat but there was literally seconds before the door closed and Frankie Lena's friend was a feet or two away "on the count of three one two three they made a massive leap which got them nearer towards the house and got in just before it shut.

The stunned couple looked stunned and very much mortified by their arrival, They sat there froze to the spot and did not move as Frankie was quick to start talking in the thought they would go if she didn't start quick enough Frankie still had the darkest and most humiliated looks on his face that everyone wanted to start chuckling. "Now guys how could you miss school everyone was asking for you there really worried" "Where just madly in love" looking at Frankies for help "Yeah madly in love we sneak out because we care about each other" "Don't you know what that feels like" Lena and Frankie looked madly into each other's eyes and didn't care they kissed. Frankie understood and before they could say a word more Frankie the 2nd one was back inside the pizza, He began to have a clearer idea of what Lena was after him doing he had to find some way of getting back to Lena and fast, Frankie was a big fan of pizza admittingly and couldn't help but want to stay but these memories were too great to ignore. He had to make sure that Lena knew that he wanted a second chance at their relationship. The orb picked out some great times they had as youngsters at school that the 10 years felt like not very much to him. He loved Lena a lot with all his heart his heart was devoted to one. Francesco this time had to think of a plan a very wise cunning plan of what he could transform into this time it was a race against the clock. There was the most minuscule of gaps up ahead where he was trapped he thought and he thought and had just the idea he scurried out as a very small with venomous teeth that could bite through skin and so it did it took out great chunks so much that the monster felt it he made his through gap by gap Francesco was doing well until the pizza ghost had a defence he put up guards defending the exit to come out. However this was no match for the great Francesco he just started biting them and when out of the monster without any further traps.

The pizza ghost started screaming and took a hard knock to the head due to how much the Francesco rat had taken off. Free pizza was available with immediate effect. Francesco had a vision that Lena was with him as he took the pizza slice Lena was right next to him ready to smooch. Francesco remembered the beauty behind Lena and with this mind carried on straight through gate number 3 but before he could enter the 3rd section. Roxanne with her mum like ways came running up towards a wall and noticed something moving and instantly knew it was him as the whole family proceeded on behind her. She broke open the wall with help and it exploded with bricks falling from the sky it was raining bricks "That was so cool" coughed Francesco he got up and heard his mom's voice and instantly hugged her they had not seen each other in a very long time he was hurt but not for long remember he could not feel injuries he was a odd individual but strangely unique. Pauline gave him a kiss on the forehead and marched him on home for all the worry that he gave her and the family. As they were heading off home Francesco continued to see Lena and wanted to grab out and reach her but she was never really that far away.

Chapter 23

EVERY LIVING THOUGHT LIES WITH LENA

Francesco continued to wake up each night with Lena on his mind he could not get him out of his mind he had a burning desire to see her again. A knock then could be heard from the window he looked around and spotted what looked like an exact replicate of Lena which it was. He rushed over to the window and spotted Lena the first thing he had to do what hug her and hug again "How did you find my puzzle of a wall there pretty interesting right" laughed Lena "It was fun but I could" he could not finish the sentence "You could not what?" he remained silent "You can tell me anything you know this even in the dreams in the wall I told you this" "Francesco a pussy" She chanted. He blushed she continued to chant these very words until he came out and let it of his chest "OK, OK, I was thinking about you and I couldn't wait to see you" "Awh that's the sweetest" She kissed him on the cheek "You know you still look handsome from the day we went on our first date" She winked. Lena showed him a pic showing that very day and went on to explain what they had it was an amazing meal "Hey do you fancy going out and doing that all over again tomorrow" "I would love to". She came around the very next day. She came in through the very traditional door that she use to enter to see him all them years ago to find Francesco crying he was over by the table she called him. He gestured her over and said it right from the heart "My mum's got cancer" "What" Francesco went on to explain that during the night after she left he had heard right from the door his dad was screaming and she seemed to be in considerable pain. It was not till the morning that his dad had the guts to tell and since then he had been crying.

Pauline had gone for several checks that morning all coming back to say that she didn't have long to live. She was now at least 58 years old and had been of big help with everything in Frankie's life. Everything from homework to supporting with plays and his career. Now 28 nearly as old Lena. Lena put her hands by his side. This was a perfect opportunity from them to find their footing and they still could go out for their planned dinner together as a whole family she invited everyone and they replayed out every seen from 10 years prior. Pauline could not have been happier to see Frankiepoo more happy in his stage of his life as she liked to call him. There were very often moments where she would ultimately break down in front of them and seek comfort from them all. Knowing very well that the cancer she had would play a big role in her life and even bigger role in making sure she spent that time with her family to the fullest.

The following day they got a influx on letters wishing them well as she ate her breakfast but was increasing ill and spent most of other times up in her room one letter reading "Dear Pauline were very sorry to hear you are ill and I do hope this is not real and that it all turns out to be fake we love and we'll be around to see you soon all the best PS: get lots of rest you'll need it" xxxxxxx. Lena was mostly with them and spent some time away but she didn't want to see Frankie go through it alone. Her key objective was to get him away from all that was happening and make him smile which they did. Lena's family was preparing to go on that holiday that they discussed earlier on in the story but they couldn't do without her there so they cancelled it and came over due to being neighbours and offered presents and to help out wherever needed. Lena's mom had a long list of jobs to do but she wasn't alone and they all made it easier on her. Everything from shopping, to ironing, to feeding the cats etc she was incredibly grateful for that. She could spend the time looking at letters she opened one to find that there was more than just a letter in there there was a toy she had when she was younger there was no name "Dear Paul shorten name for you it's very upsetting to see you are so unwell so I brought you this to make you better about yourself you had always said you wanted this so here it is enjoy and have fun we'll be around shortly stay safe stay warm and look after yourself no name" She had quite a lot of friends that it had the potential to be but she couldn't be sure who it was it was from this point to bug her all night long.

Chapter 24

PAULINE'S FRIEND RETURNS

Pauline lay in her bed wondering when she would see the person she knew gave the teddy bear she looked at it and noticed her favourite earring on and then examined the letter to find anything that might resemble this in any way there was a bit down the bottom of the page which looked like it have something to do with the description of the bear. She found a side note right at the bottom of the page and showed it to her man sitting right next door to her. He seemed to notice something very revealing about the message that with his glasses on he could see a name that Pauline could not and an address was that just a trait of his or did he have better eyesight. He repositioned himself and pointed at what he was talking about "That is where we should visit" "Tomorrow let's say" He gave her a peck on the cheek and fell into a very deep sleep. She had definitely agreed to this but felt anxiety and a fair bit of nerve going around after all these years. Twenty years passed since she last visited her her name being Florence. Florence was of them type of people who could be incredibly nervous and liked to keep herself to herself she did half expect them to follow it on from the letter after all these years but she did and brought around a far few guests with her Lena being one of them down the road of where they lived they never lived not too far away from each other it was to basically to rekindle them memories she entered and the all too well known scent of cakes being made it was one of her favourites.

 She felt cold and started shaking uncontrollably she had to have something to eat it was the time as she stand there listening to Florence. As she arrived into the kitchen she was on the floor she went on 20 years from that day it was an unforgettable moment. It was the same orange colour it was very precisely detailed with patterns of zigzags just like she remembered other patterns including but not limited to stripes they were a red with a very funky additional pattern never seen one that Florence created all by herself. She took a photo and felt it was so delicately done that it deserved at least 5-10 minutes of her attention. Florence at this exact minute came into the room and spotted Pauline looking down at her art work. "It's beautiful isn't it" she nodded and felt it only right to hug her.

They celebrated over a very friendly tea this was until Pauline collapsed on the floor she was halfway through her food when she became very pale in the face she dropped so fast that it became hard to see where she now was. The next noise you heard for was something of a vomiting one. Pauline had just been sick and was very sweaty and struggling to breath. Pauline remembered waking up a few hours later seeing a group of doctors and concerned friends and family who held her hand throughout. She was dazed and confused as she came around. She was soon to find out that the cancer she had would play a significant part in how long she had to live as they feared it was only to be a week. She began crying at the hearing of this news and had signs to prove this. Florence suggested they take a holiday in the last week you could hear her saying "No, no, I don't want to die" panic in every word she said she was frightened but Florence was at hand to help and was more than delighted to her assistance. She had a special tree at home which before the holiday she had and the rest of the family had a picnic under they spent the week doing the things that mattered most. They embarked on a holiday of a lifetime not just one but 3 to every destination she had not visited as of yet. It made her smile a tone and we wouldn't have wanted it any other way Florence would state a week later after her untimely death stating how she lost a star a true icon and a treasure to all concerned. But this was the beginning of their troubles.

Chapter 25

THE UNEXPECTED FUNERAL

After Pauline's untimely death a day or two before her 59th birthday there were very clear preparations put into place. Everything from pre-parties to other big plans to see that she would make a very joyous period of time she had on earth. The parties were very carefully planned out and had her get involved as much as possible. They even get bands Pauline's favourite it was really quite a special one. In fact to remember her by, they played that same band. Love hearts and messages were put on so heartfelt that it really moved people that came to read them. They gathered in huge crowds to see the passing of a princess or queen in their eyes. There was rigorous applause for everyone who knew her she was hugely popular and this was definitely reflected in the vast amount of people attending. They laid her to rest not long after the ceremony and talks. It was very bitter however there was constant positivity from all concerned.

A couple of days there was to be an incident to top all incidents. Francesco had originally gone to the funeral as planned but then the next day two he wasn't to be seen by anybody until today he was seen to be driving in what looked like a black Mercedes until one person on seeing what was going on saw something completely different a black Audi came to view. It was coming towards a house at top speed. Everything from the funeral looked around to find it was coming towards them and swerved away from the house with Francesco in it! Seconds later he was still heading towards the tomb where Pauline lied. Everyone tried to push him back with very little effect she rampaged past as his way was blocked he ran over them as by this point police were on his tail he gone over the soil and broke the tomb of Pauline. The police surrounded him as everyone cried and wondered why this could have happened he was still undercover pretty much as he continued to cause havoc and destruction in the town. Going through small to big houses he didn't care the look the people could see on his face was of something truly troubled ge couldn't hold in anymore. Lena when racing after him but then something made a very big bang.

Francesco wouldn't Lena live past this day forgetting this one she needed to help and she needed to help fast before time ran out. She took cover to show she was not scared and took to calling the police who were not too far away explaining how she knew Francesco and what kind of person he was. The police sped up and called more crew to the scene and had him boxed him ready to attack they drew in closer but as they did Francesco lifted up from the ground and started chucking fire missiles from his car directly at the below vehicles even Lena!. Lena started to have firm words to get him down as the whole of the town was lit up in flames. "Babe come down from there I know you have problems and we'll fix them together" "Look I know we haven't really seen eye to eye but I can help you" She continued but just then the many bombs he dropped made it too late she was too late he had caused his damage to make it even more unsavory in taste he hadn't been listening and been more interested in the police she had even been hurt he was ready to give Lena the time of her life! With more attacks coming her way.

Chapter 26

THE AFTERMATH OF THE FIGHT

The bombs were never ending he wanted to destroy Lena but what changed during the period of him getting on well with Lena and now destroying the whole of her neighbourhood. Well you see during the time that they meet and bounded and now his parents had seen Francesco and sucked some of the life that he had from the evil spirits inside him they used this and gave Francesco some evil ideas over the next couple of months they would get rid for something bigger than they expected by using his car to cause so much destruction it would be unreal. However they had one person they had their eyes on and that was Lena. Frankie had told a lot to his parents about what use to be his true love Lena, Lena was his number 1 now 15 years ago but now he seeked revenge for some unknown reason and needed the help of his dad to come up with the best idea to get rid of her there were several ideas up in the air but nothing was set in stone until one day his dad knew in the afternoon to be precise he showed Francesco the very idea and he loved it and both of them had the evil spirits after he shared with his him and gave him a quarter of his soul pretty much. This what led to the next day's atrocities it was something that the town had NOT seen before. But Francesco was ready to cause as much havoc as possible once again. But there is something that was missed from the police when they came to interview him.

Something else lied in his seat a picture of Lena and himself but this wasn't to be found out until weeks later after the incident. Lena was given a copy of this in the weeks it took to find it and she took a long glimpse over it and couldn't help but want to forgive you know the feeling but after all the trouble he caused it would not be that easy she was so upset with him right about now!. Francesco was in the police cell not long after the interview and was found to be guilty of causing harm to over citizens he vowed to continue his revengeful schemes but after the stint of evil had worn off he started to regret really quickly. He lay there upset and wanting to find ways out. Questions ran through his head he wondered why he would of done this especially when he loved Lena and the town he lived in. Although he couldn't deny he had problems that he needed to fix behind four walls. He didn't believe he knew how he enlisted help over the next couple of years but this was a far few years. Lena had recovered from her injuries to the extent they were at and also the rest of the family did as well. After the traumatic ordeal they had gone through she noticed she had not seen here friends for a very long time and had wondered where they were at these days. She walked up the very familiar pathway of the first house where her friend lived to find a very nice but somewhat heartbreaking surprise.

Chapter 27

LENA REUNITES WITH THE PAST

Lena walked up closer to the front of the door to find something she was not expecting to see something from her past she looked down at a cot like basket near the door and found a baby her baby from many years past. Although he had obtained many a serious blow from years past. Her eyes filled with a watery substance which could be tears as she looked at her child. But how did he get here? She took the baby away and took the child back home cradling him in her arms she was excited at the same time concerned. She was immediately advised to take him to the hospital and get him checked over. It was more serious than first expected he was to have received a very big blow to his facial muscles to his abdomen and to his leg. His left leg had be reduced to a scar and his abdomen had been completely destroyed it would seem he was in a lot of pain as you could see by the amount of tears he himself had running down his face. The doctor took one look and immediately sent him to the emergency room A and E, she looked through the glass hoping that he would recover she was sorry for all the years that he had not been seen after the split Frankie won the case against little baby Brady. Brady was in there for 48 hours before being considered to leave.

The doctors returned back out the doors and advised Lena to sit as it all spoken to her about and there was to it then meet the eye. She sat there and called friends over as she couldn't contain herself and seriously regret not being a bigger part of the life of her one and only. B came over to the hospital and stayed with her throughout making sure that she ate something and was looking after herself. She was allowed to come to the bedside of the children's section. It was not only B that came Camilla and Valentine did too and somehow Francesco? How could this be? How did he get out and so quick he suddenly released and had a confession to make as he had the same reaction as Lena but Lena fended him off with a physical brawl between the two of them took place shortly after. The kids section was packed with very poorly as Brady was taken over a few days later. Brady couldn't quit open his eyes which was off great worry to them both but Lena still continued to fend him off and ultimately get into a second fight with him they couldn't not be together and only Lena knew this. Lena was upset but still loved him so how. So much so that evening they were talking and got back together getting incredibly loved up she couldn't resist the charms even this long after their relationship ended 15 years prior but after not getting of the child Francesco made his intentions very clear. They had a very in depth chat about what they wanted and agreed they would go back to court. He even shouted during the whole chat to stand his ground it turned physical again. He just a fetish of being nasty and lashing out given the chance but was that just him? Or was it that thing he had always said took over him? They went their separate ways but weeks later came that time to find out the answer to the question he had always wanted answer to who was better having the child as Lena knew she was the best but didn't have custody of him so it was one against the other one story against the other who would win who would lose Lena was determined she walked in and it all was to off started very quickly without any further delay

Chapter 28

THE COURT HEARING

The court hearing was to been in progression from 10 ock thursday morning with ups and some very big setbacks Lena was in one side of the court and Francesco was on the other side arguing his case making sure he won with Lena doing the same. To make sure he lost she put on the strongest scent with it wafting into his nose causing him to say something completely different to what he would normally say and he wore the most colourful jewellery ever for example his watch he loved that watch and could not wait to shine in her face, this was to get a head-ups on Lena who he knew would win if he was not to of done this. The judge looked on and saw this happening and put a very immediate stop to this "stop" they were still brawling after this announcement he raised his voice and ran out and tapped their tables "Shut the fuck up" they looked around the judge and sad immediately silenced but then still spoke but spoke in a lowered tone, which was preferred for all, the judge began by getting both sides of the story they were very mixed and somewhat confusing. The whole of the rest of the audience had been split as to what side to take.

As they proceeded on further throughout the afternoon it became more complicated to find a conclusion. But they had to find some way of finding an answer so the judge made a judgement call and there was only way to go with Francesco, Lena stood there stunned knowing they wouldn't not be together any further. Lena had lost it all as she went towards the floor falling into a very deep depression shortly after that and Francesco ran out and had a very clear plan ahead as he partied the night away. But had Francesco planned this it was all over so quick or was it a dream. The world became a dark one once again and he took over the world with Brady in his every thought and his plans would involve him too but in a good way as Lena walked out after a few days and saw nothing more of them she had this idea to go ahead with but then she picked up a newspaper and her son had just done the most heroic thing ever. This led her to say "that's my boy" her whole perception on Francesco changed dramatically she had to go and tell her how she felt over such an amazing thing her son had done in 24 hours! The quest begun she would be thrilled to what would be seen outside when she entered the outside world miracles do come true.

Chapter 29

BRADY BECOMES SUPERHERO

I walked outside to find bright lights and the sun shining brighter than ever. The whole town was fixed from its original state the whole path was a gold colour the sun was beaming down on it. There was now a beach added to the town Lena took no hesitation on spending time relaxing on it but who did something like this? She heard news from the residents that a boy named Brady did such things. Brady came down from his superhero duties with Francesco travelling with him and called "mum" "my baby" however before he could go a bit further there were certain rules that had to be followed. He had a folder in his hands which had a document she had to look at which had rules to which she had to follow it read "Lena you're not allowed within 5 feet of Theo you cannot see him unless in the company of Francesco" she felt heartbroken "With expressed permission from Francesco you can come around to see him" but the custody will always be his under no grounds can this be changed unless something changes and you are to see eye to eye again" Lena observed the parchment and didn't feel she could forgive and forget after all the shit she went through with Francesco it seems very difficult and didn't feel right, not giving a care in the world she went down on her heels came in closer and said "I love you Theo I always will" but I can't see you be the man you will become but I will always fight for you whatever happens never forget I will always be with you in here she pointed towards his heart, Lena's tears turned out to Brady's tears he didn't want to see Lena cried and ended up not caring and ended up not caring, Francesco used his push-away charm and pushed Lena away, "you have to get use to this" "He's mine you had your chance" but they ignored and still embraced their love was too powerful it was too great.

Francesco tried pushing Lena away endlessly but there was nothing he could do this was till he smacked Lena on the head and she became unconsciousness bearing in mind it had been half an hour that he allowed this to happen, Theo kneeled down but Francesco had the upper hand and took his hand and got him away "you're mine now your mum is no longer a part of your life I'm sorry" he showed very little remorse "remember we have to save the world together he couldn't forget her and they got back to his to find that he went into a state of depression himself he took a lot of alcohol and begun smoking it seemed unreal he wanted his mum back. One night Francesco took his eye of the ball as Theo took of out of his cote and went in search to be the superhero for his mum his one and only love like they were. He weren't giving up he would search all night as he crawled through the grassy fields and the many cities. Lena had to be somewhere but it was a question of where?

Chapter 30

THE THINGS YOU DO FOR LOVE

The things you do for love are incredible and this baby had a big love for his mum understable but he had to find her. The grassy patches went on and on and on for some time and it got bigger. He brought them all down. As Frankie was still puffing away on his cigarette unawares. Lena had got up and had felt something was coming to find her so she went running as the Theo made noises over the other noises and traffic, he would do anything for his mum his dad not so his irresponsible ways really begun to show he crawled through alleyways up pipes and was brave at all times. Lena wouldn't want any different at all she always wanted her child to see the world and really make himself known. He wasn't going to let her down as the crawling and walking took place people stopped and took a moment just to look at a baby doing this. In his baby voice which was understood by many after his dad's and his self's heroic act from earlier really showed how much of an amazing kid he was they cheered this way every town and city they helped him as he took to the sky and looked down as he tried to tracked down his mum he then saw something. A shape with his eyes anything was possible he was so relieved but when he got down it wasn't what he had bargained for something else meet the toddler's eyes.